C000229198

PJ Hammond is best knowr
cult science-fiction series *Sa*
Lumley and David McCallu
television in the 1970's after working as a script editor and
writer on *Z-Cars*. His extensive writing credits also include
The Sweeney, *The Bill* and *Midsomer Murders*, plus sci-fi and
fantasy series *Ace of Wands* and *Shadows* for Thames TV and
Sky TV's *Space Island One*.

Hammond was approached to write for *Doctor Who* in
the 1980's, however his story *Paradise Five* was eventually
recorded as a full cast audio drama starring the sixth doctor,
Colin Baker, as part of the *'Lost Stories'* season. Hammond
also penned two episodes of the *Doctor Who* spin-off series
Torchwood.

DOWNTIMERS

PJ HAMMOND

First published as a paperback in 2018

ISBN 978-1-9999685-0-2

Text copyright © PJ Hammond 2018
Cover image copyright © PJ Hammond 2018

Published by Scarsmoor Publishing

Design and typesetting by Inkyeverafter Press
www.inkyeverafterpress.com

For my dear, late brother, John,
who urged me to write Downtimers

Prologue

They came for him at three-thirty in the afternoon.
The afternoon of his wedding day. The wedding of
fifty-one year old David Doughty, a stranger to the
area, and Annette Smith, 'spinster of this parish'.

There were only a few well-wishers at the
ceremony. There was Annette's younger, married
sister, their aged mother, and three of Annette's
work colleagues. But there was no-one to represent
Doughty because he knew no-one apart from his
wife-to-be. Annette's mother was prevailed upon
to be the witness. And with no best man, the
registrar's assistant volunteered to stand beside
Doughty and hold the wedding ring.

It was a reasonably warm day in late September.
Thankfully, the morning rain had cleared and the
sun was now shining.

Sol Bonner and John Pierce waited outside the

registry office. They watched as Doughty led his dearly beloved to the ribbon bedecked hire car that Annette had insisted upon having. Bonner held a small paper bag of rose petals. He reached out and scattered the petals over the happy couple. The bride smiled a thank you. Bonner and Pierce then informed Doughty that he was wanted for questioning.

David Doughty, a fugitive from another place and another time, would never see his wife again.

1

Gate Town was a crap town. Almost everyone thought that. But there were those who cared about the place, who were brought up there, who didn't mind its backdrop of heavy industry, mostly in decline, and its featureless streets.

The flat was situated not far from the town centre. It was not the kind of property that one would wish to live in for too long. It was shabby. It was bleak. It was a passing-through place.

A child of four years old was waiting in the cramped sitting room. She wore a winter coat. She was sleepy. A full backpack of belongings and a carrier bag containing a few toys had been placed by the door.

From outside, the ceaseless sound of traffic could be heard from the street. It was just after seven-forty-five p.m. on a Friday evening in mid

November.

The child's mother entered the room. She was buttoning her outdoor coat. She was probably in her mid thirties. She looked pale and tired. But she was pretty. She had been using the name Eve Palmer. Her daughter had been allowed the name Cara.

The woman gave the briefest of smiles as she hugged the child and held her close for a moment before releasing her.

'Time to go,' the woman said.

Detective Inspector Bonner had never enjoyed his wife Lesley's supper parties. He simply suffered them. And here he was again on this cold November evening, sitting down to eat with the same people that Lesley always seemed determined to invite. There was the deadly dull couple from across the street, plus Lesley's prick of a brother and his wife.

Bonner was forty-four years old. He was about five feet ten, well built and with a slightly battered look about him. He had been an everyday CID sergeant for some years and was more or less content with that. But now, with his sudden panic promotion to a small, special and newly organised unit, there was more money coming in, which made life easier.

The prick of a brother was having a rant about the threat of dangerous illegal immigrants possibly living in the area, and the general public being urged to report anything or anyone that aroused their suspicions.

Bonner had a smile to himself. It was his department that had put out the disguised warning. He was glad to see it was working.

Pierce was watching and waiting outside the Palmers' flat. In contrast to Bonner, he was a tall, thin man, well over six feet in height. And he wore Buddy Holly glasses. He stirred and shifted his position as Eve Palmer and her daughter emerged from the building.

In Bonner's house his brother-in-law was still in full-cry.

'We don't want any more immigrants anyway. Legal or not legal. This country can't take any more. I mean, we're not exactly a large nation, are we? We could probably fit into the state of California. And with room to spare...'

As ever, Bonner let it all wash over him. If he had his way he'd never have a supper party or a lunch party or any kind of fucking party where people just sat and talked about sod all. He'd rather be in a pub, or simply sitting at home with his feet up and a glass or two of scotch inside him. But Lesley liked her little get-togethers, as she called them. And Bonner respected that. He didn't really fancy her any more. But then again he wasn't allowed to. Not these days. But she was kind and he cared about her. So he reckoned this is probably all you get when you end up living in a fairly reasonable semi, in a passable residential street – although there weren't too many of those in Gate Town – with your mortgage payments almost completed. You get this. For the rest of your sodding life.

'So what are you up to these days, Sol?'

Mrs. Deadly Dull, God bless her, had decided to shut the prick up by changing the subject.

'Been promoted again, have you?'

'No. Just the one promotion's enough,' said Bonner. 'That'll do me'.

Mr. Deadly Dull joined in, 'Lesley says you're probably doing some special work at the moment, with all the odd hours you put in.'

'Me? No. Just good old honest police work.'

Lesley gave a vague but contented smile. 'He doesn't tell me anything. And I never ask.'

'Best way, love,' said Bonner.

Eve and Cara Palmer walked along the litter strewn

street. To them it seemed a threatening place, with each passing stranger or lurking figure possibly capable of violence. Shops and business premises had shutters or security grills in place. Vehicles continued to drive past, to and fro, non-stop. Eve held Cara's hand. The backpack was slung over her shoulder. With her free hand she clutched the carrier bag of toys.

A heavy lorry swung out from a side street and revved and clattered its way past them, much too close to them. Eve pulled her daughter tightly to her, as if to protect her from all the sights and sounds of this ugly world. They walked on along the street.

John Pierce followed Eve and the child. But not at a discreet distance. There was no need for that.

Pierce had been with UK Immigration for most of his working life, but had recently been seconded, at short notice, to CID. He had also been allowed to 'borrow' the rank of detective inspector.

Up ahead, the lights of a police station could be seen.

Mrs. Bonner and her sister were gathering up dirty plates as Bonner reached for the brandy bottle. His mobile rang. He excused himself, got up from the table and moved out into the hallway. He reached for the phone which was on the hall table.

'Yep?'

Pierce was on the line. 'They've come out of the house. Both of them. With luggage.'

'Heading where?'

'To Prior Street nick.'

'Christ!'

'It's all right. As a precaution I've just called their duty sergeant and briefed him. He'll deal if he has to'.

'What did you tell him?'

'A lie, of course.' Pierce sounded offended. 'What did you think I'd tell him?'

'OK. Send for the team.'

'Already done that.'

Bonner grabbed his coat.

Someone had puked up on the front steps of the police station. A car cruised by, windows down even in the cold air, boom-box base blaring, boom-di-di-boom-di-di-boom as Eve and her daughter stepped carefully around the pool of spew.

The police station was a left-over from the fifties so-called contemporary architecture. It was now a grubby looking place that had dated badly.

In the front office reception area a couple of pissed-off looking black youths were sprawled across a bench while their mother shouted the odds about a problem neighbour to a WPC who was at the open hatch of the front desk. Coppers moved to and fro with the self-locking communicating door slamming shut behind them each time. Those entering had to wait for the WPC to push a button and buzz them in.

Eve struggled in from the street with Cara and the luggage. The child stumbled and Eve had to drop the backpack to grab at her. She saw a crude felt-pen sign taped to the side of the hatch which read 'Please sit down and wait until you are called.' She looked around her for somewhere to sit and wait but there was only the fully occupied bench. The youths weren't hostile. It was just that they weren't going to move for anyone. That wouldn't have made sense to them. They watched idly as Eve straightened the backpack. She sat Cara upon it. The child was now half asleep. Eve crouched down to attend to her as the youths' mother continued her futile rant about justice, while all around phones rang, buzzers buzzed, doors slammed, and somewhere, deep in the locked-up heart of this place, there was the hellish sound of someone intermittently crying and singing.

Pierce was standing outside the police station. He checked his watch. He took a pair of protective gloves from his pocket. He proceeded to roll on the gloves. He looked along the street.

Inside the building, the youths' mother had given up her losing battle with the law for the time being. Shouting that she wasn't finished yet and she'd be back, don't you worry about that, she left with her two grinning sons in tow. At the same time a thick set, traffic officer veteran entered and was buzzed through the communicating door to have a loud laugh and a joke with the WPC. Eve was ignored as the police activity sounds continued unabated. But Cara seemed comfortable on the backpack while her mother gazed at the information posters pinned to the walls

'Can I help you?'

Eve looked up to see the WPC watching her through the hatch. Behind her, the traffic cop could be seen filling out a form. Eve gathered Cara up in her arms and moved to the desk. She looked into the soulless eyes of the WPC and said, 'We don't belong here.'

'Don't belong where? In Gate Town?'

'That's right.'

'OK.' The WPC reached for a notepad. 'What's your name? And where are you from?'

'We're from the future,' said Eve.

A uniformed duty sergeant had appeared from

the interior with some paperwork. He stopped as he saw Eve at the desk.

'The future? Never heard of 'em,' said the WPC. 'So what are they? Some kind of insurance company?'

Eve spoke patiently but wearily. 'We're from another place in time. Years and years from now.'

The WPC looked up from the notepad. The traffic officer was grinning. 'Boy, do we get 'em!' he said.

At that moment Pierce entered the reception area. The duty sergeant saw him. He moved quickly as he shouted an order to the WPC. 'I want 'em in here.'

The WPC was puzzled. 'Sarge?'

'Custody suite. I want them in there. Now.' He grabbed a set of keys, tossed them to the WPC, then buzzed open the communicating door. As he and the WPC emerged from the front office Eve looked suspiciously at the tall figure of Pierce, who was calmly watching her. 'This way, love,' said the sergeant, taking Eve by the arm.

Still holding Cara, Eve turned to her backpack and carrier bag. 'But our things...'

'Don't worry about them,' said Pierce. Eve gave him another wary look as she and Cara were led away.

Outside the building an SUV had arrived carrying an Army M.O. and a paramedic. Both were wearing protective kit. The M.O. grabbed his bag from the vehicle as an unmarked but fully equipped police van parked behind the SUV. Two security officers climbed from the van.

Inside the police station the traffic cop and other officers stood looking baffled as Pierce and his team invaded the front office. Pierce was carrying Eve's backpack and carrier bag. 'They're in the cell block,' he said to the M.O.

As the medical team moved towards the custody suite Pierce peered inside the backpack. He then opened the carrier bag. It contained a couple of dolls, some small toys, a colouring book and a plastic, tube shaped case of coloured pencils. 'Bag this lot,' he said to his security men.

The desk sergeant had returned and was curious about what was going on. 'You said on the phone they could be terrorists. They look nothing like terrorists.'

Pierce ignored the man as he watched his team deal with the backpack and carrier bag.

Unlike the WPC and the traffic cop, the desk sergeant seemed a rather more caring individual. 'And one of them's just a child,' he protested.

Pierce continued with his lie. 'I know,' he said.

'They start 'em young these days.'

2

Ferry Lane was in the most run-down business section of Gate Town. Not that there was a ferry any more. That disappeared when the river silted up, well over a hundred years ago. There were industrial units, unprepossessing office buildings, and fenced-off lorry parks. One could hear the sounds and see the lights of vehicles passing almost non-stop on the stretch of overpass that spanned the dried-up creek. But at least Ferry Lane boasted one pub. It was called the Old Gantry Inn, known simply as the Gantry by the locals.

Sol Bonner parked his modest, dark blue hatchback outside the pub.

Henrietta O'Day was enjoying a laugh and a joke at the bar as she sipped her second gin and tonic of the evening. She was a round, plump woman who always dressed immaculately. No-one really knew her age. Bonner had always thought she was in her mid-fifties. Pierce reckoned she could have been older. Not that it really mattered to them. She was now their boss and she was different to any other boss either of them had worked under, and she was a fucking sight better. She lived in the Ferry Lane area and had never considered leaving the place. It suited her. She wore a wedding ring but no-one could remember having seen her husband. In fact, Bonner and Pierce had never heard her mention him. So they didn't ask. They daren't.

The Gantry was a real pub. It wasn't an eating pub. You could buy crisps, pickled eggs, a warmed up pasty or pie, and that was your lot. And the Gantry should have been a smoking pub. It deserved to have filled ashtrays and air that fussy non-smokers could hardly breathe in. But that wasn't allowed any more. It had a dartboard and a pool table, and the customers were mostly men. Gathered at the bar with Mrs. O'Day were some manual workers and a few sad looking, late-leaving-the-office geeks.

The landlord of the pub was an overweight man with eyes like purple grapes and a serious, but controlled, drink problem. His name was George, and he rarely moved his arse from a stool that was positioned behind the bar. It was the full-time barman, Clumpy Ron, who did all the work.

Bonner entered the pub. He moved to join Mrs. O'Day at the end of the bar. The customers were now doing bloke talk as they discussed routes and roads and makes of cars.

Mrs. O'Day reached for her purse. 'What are you having, Sol?'

'Nothing. There isn't time.'

He seemed a little edgy. Mrs. O'Day saw the look. 'What is it?'

Bonner moved closer to her and spoke quietly as a couple of the customers argued the merits of the M20 motorway. 'That woman and child in the flat. They left home. With luggage. Tried to give themselves up.'

Mrs. O'Day stared at him. 'Fucking hell!' She picked up her drink. She downed it in one.

Bonner led the way out from the pub and into the cold night air. 'We've been watching and waiting as planned, hoping she might lead us to some others, maybe to the father of the kid. But no. She walked straight into Prior Street nick. Told those donkeys in there they were from the future.'

'Well, at least she's admitted it.'

'Yeah.'

As Bonner unlocked his car a young prostitute called Jace crossed the road on the way to the pub.

She was dressed in a mini-skirt and a pale blue PVC coat. As she passed the car she gave Bonner a great big Marilyn Monroe smile and blew him a kiss. Bonner smiled back at her. Mrs. O'Day was unimpressed with the friendly exchange.

Bonner's car drove onto the overpass and above Ferry Lane. Mrs. O'Day had wound down her window and was smoking a fag.

'They've been in that flat how long?'

'Since mid May. By my calculations the fella we nicked at the registry office must have downtimed not long after.'

'And yet they've never met.'

'Not as far as we can make out, no.'

The name downtimers had been given to people like Eve and Cara and David Doughty. All three had gone undetected before a fourth visitor from the future arrived in Gate Town. But this latest traveller was found dead on arrival, and it was his manner of death and the subsequent post-mortem result that had set the warning bells ringing.

Mrs. O'Day threw the butt of her cigarette out of the car window. 'So how the fuck do they travel back in time? And why would they want to come to Gate Town of all places? They could have gone to an area of outstanding natural beauty, like

Stevenage.'

Bonner grinned as Mrs. O'Day fiddled with the window power switch.

'With all your money, Sol, why don't you buy a better fucking car?'

'What money?' said Bonner as he eased the car onto the dual carriageway and picked up speed.

Before taking early retirement, Mrs. O'Day was once Chief Superintendent of the south east division of the Ministry of Defence Police. When she decided to leave she was badly missed because there was nothing phoney, pretentious or over ambitious about her, and she could walk and talk with the people. And whenever fools were expected to be suffered, she was always last in the queue. She had been instrumental in helping to solve cases as wide ranging as Ministry of Defence leaks, terrorist threats, and in-house military crimes and linked suicides. She had drunk champagne with naff celebrities who wanted to cosy up with members of parliament. She had been interviewed on TV by interviewers who were not, and never would be, the masters of their subject. She had even shaken hands with Bob Geldoff. But then she grew tired of the bureaucracy, and the whingers, and the protesters, and all those back-stabbing bastards who were just out for themselves.

Early retirement had meant a smaller pension, but it was enough for Mrs. O'Day. So she gave up the job in order to live quietly in Gate Town with her gin and tonics and her potted plants. Until now, when she was brought back in a hurry and offered good money and all the help she felt was necessary.

Bonner's car travelled out of Gate Town for just over six miles. It then turned off the main highway a short distance before the build-up of traffic caused by major road widening works up ahead. It was a nightmare construction operation that seemed to have been going on for months and had left the landscape looking like a dust covered battlefield and would do little to improve Gate Town and its environs.

The car bumped its way along a dark, uneven and deserted track road.

'That tart in the blue coat,' said Mrs. O'Day.

'She's just a friend.'

'I thought she was a self-harmer.'

'She was. But she's got over it.'

Mrs. O'Day wasn't totally convinced. She glanced at Bonner. 'And you're messing around with her? I mean, the slag can't be more than seventeen.'

'She's twenty-two. She fools everyone.'

'Well, I suppose that keeps the punters happy.'

21

Bonner said nothing.

'Just don't fuck up on me, Sol. We don't need that.'

'I won't,' said Bonner as the car reached the security gates of an illuminated, fenced-off establishment.

Charnham Cross had been built early in the twentieth century and had served as a military corrective training camp, or glasshouse, for the two world wars. Since then it had remained with the M.O.D. and put to various uses such as storage and training. But it had been abandoned for the past twelve years and was now earmarked for demolition as part of the construction work. But as it was close to Gate Town, Mrs. O'Day had managed to change all that, and Charnham Cross was now hers to be used as a detention centre for as long as she needed.

John Pierce was waiting as Bonner's car drove through the manned gates and parked outside what was once the administration building. Mrs. O'Day and Bonner climbed from the car.

Pierce was as coldly efficient and fully informed as ever. 'The M.O. has got a lot more examinations to make. But for the time being he's passed them fit to be here.'

Mrs. O'Day nodded. She walked towards the admin building entrance. A waiting security officer opened the door for her.

Mrs. O'Day's team was made up of carefully selected police and military security and medical personnel. She had seconded Bonner from the divisional CID department on previous occasions because of his dogged, no-nonsense method of investigation. Like her, he was a Gate Town resident, happy to be one, and not in the least bit interested in mixing with all the sycophants and golf playing tossers within the various forces.

Pierce was also a local man whose work with Immigration had been of great help to Mrs. O'Day in the past. There appeared to be nothing and no-one in Pierce's life apart from his job. He was a detail freak who had an uncanny instinct for spotting things that were a little off-centre and not quite as they should be. In the present circumstances, the abilities and local knowledge of both men was ideal for Mrs. O'Day.

With long strides, Pierce led the way along slightly dilapidated, echoing corridors. He carried a large set of keys.

Charnham Cross had been given a fast and furious makeover after the first confirmed downtimer had been found dead on some waste ground close to Gate Town's cemetery. A temporary mortuary had been set up and Mrs. O'Day had ensured that the local pathologist and coroner took no part in the proceedings. She had sent for a military pathologist, whom she knew and could trust, to perform a post mortem examination of the body.

It was believed that the dead man was between twenty-eight and thirty years old and was in possession of what first appeared to be genuine documents and currency. But what had first puzzled the pathologist were the pale, perfectly formed check patterned squares on parts of his body. And it was the subsequent post mortem investigation that revealed the scar tissues were a result of what appeared to have been highly sophisticated repair work made on bone, muscle and organs at earlier stages in his life. There was also evidence of transplant operations involving human, synthetic and possibly animal parts. Mrs. O'Day had been informed that such advanced and intricate surgical work could never have taken place in the present-day.

'I couldn't put them in a cell,' said Pierce as he and the others reached a solid looking metal door.' Not a mother and child. So I've had them fixed up in a side ward in the old hospital wing for now,' He proceeded to unlock the door. 'And I managed to find a nurse to help with the kid.'

'What kind of nurse?' asked Mrs. O'Day.

'She's from the Medical Corps, attached to the Military Police. Has no immediate family. She was a pediatric nurse before she joined the service.'

Mrs. O'Day was satisfied with this.

A surveillance camera picture showed that there was a single adult bed and a child's bed in the side ward, plus a table and two chairs. There was also a small alcove with washing facilities. Cara was asleep in the child's bed. She clutched a doll. Eve Palmer was sitting at the table. She wore a category A prison jumpsuit. She looked tired and disorientated.

Bonner, Mrs. O'Day and Pierce were inside what was once the hospital observation room. They were watching the surveillance picture on a screen. The Palmers' clothes and other items, safe inside exhibit bags, were labelled and arranged on a built-in desk unit.

'We've let the child keep her own clothes and one of her dolls,' said Pierce. 'I managed to get a quick check done on all of her toys and the clothes we've allowed her to wear. They're authentic. Probably bought locally.' He indicated the exhibit bags. 'But we're not sure about the rest of their clothing. Probably travelled back with them. I've arranged to have all their kit analysed overnight.'

Mrs. O'Day continued to watch the screen. 'What's the kid's name again?'

'Cara. Her mum tells us she's four years old. Their second name is Palmer.'

Pierce reached for one of the exhibit bags. It contained receipts, letters, items of ID, and other bits of paperwork. 'But they may not be their real names,' he said as he handed the bag to Bonner. 'All their personal stuff is probably fake, like the dead downtimer's stuff, and David Doughty's.'

'Whether it's their real names or not doesn't really matter, does it?' said Bonner as he studied the items through the clear polythene of the exhibit bag. 'We've got no way of checking it out. We deal with the present and the past. Not the fucking future.'

Mrs. O'Day continued to watch the mother and daughter. 'What else did she say?'

'Not a lot at the moment,' said Pierce. 'It's like the old 'name, rank and number only' routine. But she did say they're from the year two-thousand-one-hundred-and-twenty-one. Same date that our Mr. Doughty gave us.'

On the screen, Eve had fallen forward onto

the table top, her head resting on her folded arms. Mrs. O'Day watched mother and sleeping child for a moment or two more. She then got up from her chair. 'Let them sleep,' she said, as she moved to the door. 'I want dear mum wide awake tomorrow. She's got questions to answer.'

John Pierce led the way back from the hospital wing, then on towards the partly lit, iron-meshed gantry of the cell block.

David Doughty was sitting alone in his confinement quarters, which were nothing more than two small cells that had been knocked into one. Nevertheless, it was reasonably comfortable with its bed, chair, table and washing area. But there were no newspapers or magazines, and no TV set or radio. Doughty listened as Pierce, Bonner and Mrs. O'Day's footsteps echoed their way along the gantry, then on and on until a distant metal door was opened and then clanged shut, followed by complete silence.

It was late when Bonner and Mrs. O'Day drove back to Ferry Lane. Bonner dropped his boss off outside her apartment block. It was an old converted Victorian building that was once a shipping warehouse in the days of sail and steam. By Gate Town standards it was an up-market residence, despite the fact that further similar warehouse conversions had been put on hold some time back when the developers ran out of funds.

Bonner arrived home to find Lesley still up and about. She had cleared away the supper things and washed up. She was now wearing a passion-killer dressing gown and comfortable slippers as she stood waiting for the kettle to boil.

Lesley was two years younger than Bonner, but not that long ago, and for some unknown reason, she had made up her mind to grow old much earlier than necessary. The transition had begun with Lesley suddenly telling Bonner that sex was silly at their age. He had argued that they were only in their forties for fuck's sake, or for lack of fuck's sake, but to no avail. Then she began to move in a slower, older way, and to think older thoughts and wear older women's clothes. A little later, as if part of some weird subconscious wish-fulfillment, her body decided to join in. The menopause arrived in a hurry, followed by vaginal atrophy. In other words, she dried up.

Still protesting at the abrupt loss of his love life, Bonner was sent by Lesley to the local chemist to buy a tube of lubrication gel. Sadly, it was all pointless because the lubrication treatment didn't work. Lesley found the gel cold and unpleasant, and he had found it to be a complete turn-off. From then on, they had slept in separate rooms. But Lesley was quite happy with her new-found oldness. It had made her contented.

Bonner watched Lesley as she poured hot water into a mug. She smiled at him. 'I'm making cocoa. Would you like some?'

Bonner smiled back at her. 'No thanks, love.' He walked into the dining room, poured himself a large scotch and decided that he could just as well be living with his old mum, God rest her soul.

It was midnight and the light in David Doughty's quarters automatically switched to dimmer. He was now aware that others had been brought here. He had heard them. Heard a child's voice.

For yet another night he knew he would find it difficult to sleep while his mind was forever running through the same old questions and coming up with very few of the right answers. As a potential downtimer, he had been instructed well in advance not to tell friends or relatives about this so-called trip of a lifetime. Not that that would have been possible. He had no relatives and very few close friends. But now he was asking himself had there been someone to confide in, would that someone have advised him not to do it, told him not to travel back, not to tamper with time because it doesn't belong to us? And would he have listened?

Doughty was not a believer in God, but now he found himself wondering if some almighty was punishing him for his stupidity. But then again, what about the love that he had experienced for such a short time while being here? Had it not been worth it for that? There was also the peace and contentment he had found, and the things of rare, natural beauty that existed in this otherwise ugly and menacing town, trees and shrubs and flowers that were not synthetically produced, but grew and flourished and died as nature had intended. And there was the rich, pure soil, filled with tiny living creatures, most of which had been eliminated or genetically replaced in his world.

But most important of all there was the woman he had met and grown to love, and who had become his bride. What about her feelings? Had they told her the truth about him? Not that there was much for them to learn.

And so the thoughts kept on troubling him as he lay awake in the semi-darkness of this wretched place. They had told him that he would be locked away forever. And he was sure they meant it. So, by coming here had he exchanged one kind of hell for another?

Bonner and Pierce had questioned him at Charnham Cross immediately after his arrest. His wedding suit, carnation spray and polished shoes had been taken from him and he had been dressed in category A clothes. They told him they had been watching him for some time, hoping he would provide them with visual clues on how he had arrived.

'How did you manage it?' Bonner had asked. 'How did you travel back in time?' When he had failed to answer, Bonner had persisted. 'Just fucking tell us, will you? What was the process? How is it done?'

'I can't answer that,' Doughty had managed to reply. 'I was asleep when it happened. One can only travel back during sleep.'

It was a lie but he knew his questioners could never prove otherwise. Now, in his confinement quarters, he pondered on that conversation. One thing's for certain, he told himself. Whatever else happens, they must never know the truth. They must never find out how we get here.

3

Mrs. O'Day had always been an early riser. And here she was, at six thirty in the morning, making herself a pot of coffee in the designer kitchen of her smart flat. She had always wanted a bespoke kitchen and now she had one. As well as her pension she had always been careful with her savings. She also had few ties in life. Her only responsibilities at the moment were her home and this temporary job. And for enjoyment she had her plants, her favourite framed prints, her pieces of bric-a-brac, her gin and tonics and her fags.

Ferry Lane also had its regular early starts. HGV's could be heard manoeuvring in the lorry parks and a mobile crane had started up in one of the scrap metal yards. Fairly soon these would be joined by the sounds of demolition work that was taking place on a couple of the old buildings in the area.

Mrs. O'Day carried her coffee into the living room. The panoramic window area belied the outside grot of Ferry Lane by being the next best thing to a garden room with its array of foliage and house plants. She lit her first cigarette of the morning and moved amongst the various ivies, ferns and palms to look out of the window at a cold and overcast day. And, as she surveyed the cheerless landscape, she asked herself the same question that she had asked Bonner. Why Gate Town? Why would these people from the future want to come here? What brings them here? She knew full well that if the last downtimer had not choked to death in transit he and the others would still have been living amongst us. But why were they here?

Exercise time at Charnham Cross was a supervised walk around a tarmacked compound that was surrounded by a high, chain link fence. As the only living internee, David Doughty had had the walk to himself, up until now. But last night he had heard the others, whoever they were, so this morning he took a careful look around him as he was led into the yard.

'Are there others here?' he asked his guard.

'Others like me?'

'Don't know, mate.'

'Only I'm sure I heard people arriving. Last night.'

'Ask Mrs. O'Day,' said the guard as he locked the gate. 'Maybe she can tell you.'

Doughty knew he was being lied to, as usual. But he nodded a thank you all the same as he began his lonely walk around the compound. As ever, he stopped to look at and admire a couple of distant trees. The wind picked at the branches and blew around the scattered dead leaves left over from the summer. His summer. He continued his walk. He then stopped once more and picked up one of the dry, brown leaves that had blown onto the tarmac. He studied the leaf. Then, as he looked up, he noticed something at a distance.

Beyond the compound, on a stretch of pathway bordered by a grass verge, he could see a small girl walking. The child was holding a doll. A uniformed nurse walked with her. The child turned and moved to the verge. She stepped carefully on to the grass. She tested the grass with her feet. She laughed. She jumped up and down on the grass.

A child? Doughty asked himself. A child is being kept here? In this place? Why?

Still at a distance, Cara turned. She saw

Doughty. She stared at him. Doughty raised a tentative hand. He waved. Cara waved back at him. The nurse then moved swiftly. She reached out and took Cara's hand. She led her on along the pathway.

Doughty continued to watch as Cara and the nurse moved on and out of sight.

Annette Smith had just turned thirty-nine years old when she first met David Doughty. This had been in June. She worked in Gate Town's public library and he began to visit almost every other day, not to borrow books, but to read them. He would sit in the reading area for long periods, poring over reference books and back copies of local newspapers and periodicals. During that time they had got to know each other and chatted. She had even found herself looking forward to his library visits. They had then started to go out together.

Annette lived in a small, terraced house in Gate Town. The house belonged to her elderly mother who was now in a care home. Annette's younger sister was an irritating woman who had never gone out of her way to make much of an effort in life yet had managed to gain the most from it. At the age of thirty she was on her second marriage and was also managing quite successfully to juggle a fairly lively affair.

Annette's pickiness about men, and her failure to find the right one, had always been a source of amusement to her sibling, resulting in feelings of edginess in Annette. Then along came David. And her life had changed. Within six weeks they were engaged and Doughty had moved out of his B&B to live with Annette. The house was small, and although it had a paved back yard, it lacked a proper garden. But they were happy. And she was determined to be married before she reached forty. Then, as far as she was concerned, her sister could go screw herself.

There were times when Annette wondered how her dear David managed to survive financially without a job. Yet he had money. Always had cash. They were savings, he had said. Also, she was quite happy to go Dutch, especially as he intended to work. He was eager to get a job where he could work with the good earth, as he put it, and with plants. Not easy in Gate Town, they had realised that, but something was sure to come up.

Meanwhile, Annette had spent whatever free time she had walking with her husband-to-be in nearby Providence Park. Being blighted by litter and vandalism, it was not the most attractive of places, but he loved it there. He loved the trees and the plants and the shrubs and the fish in the murky, artificial pond. Now and again he would use words that she didn't quite understand or had never heard of. When she had asked him about this he apologised, then explained that he'd been abroad for many years, therefore his language was sometimes somewhat bastardized.

During one of their walks, Annette was aware of two men sharing the same pathway for what seemed to her a considerable length of time. One was very tall indeed, and the other was shorter and stockier. Then, on another occasion, she imagined she'd seen the tall man passing by her house. But she had dismissed the thought and didn't consider it worth mentioning to David.

At the very end of September the great day came. That sunny, happy day of all days. Her big, big, wonderful day.

And the same two men were there outside the registry office. Only this time they weren't just passing by. They were waiting.

John Pierce was aged forty-one and for all of his adult years he had been a solitary soul who had never owned a home of his own, preferring to move from one rented property to another whenever he felt that his very private and uncomplicated way of life was being intruded upon. He would sometimes drink in the Gantry with Mrs. O'Day, but only if he were ordered to. Bonner had invited him to his home on a couple of occasions, for lunch or supper, but Pierce always found an excuse not to go. So Bonner eventually gave up on this.

Like Mrs. O'Day and Bonner, Pierce was also happy living in Gate Town. And he was fortunate enough to have found accommodation that suited his modest needs, and had been living there untroubled for almost a year. A record for him. He lived in a small, third floor flat above a corner shop on the south side of Gate Town. It was a multi-cultural area and Pierce's shopkeeper-landlord and his family were from Bangladesh.

Pierce always kept his flat clean. But then it had no chance of being untidy anyway, even if it wanted to, because Pierce was the ultimate minimalist whose only possessions were the things he needed on a day to day basis. He had no time for ornaments or memorabilia.

The shop below was a godsend for Pierce. It was friendly and it was open fourteen hours a day, seven days a week. Everything Pierce needed was just downstairs. There was a cash machine. He could buy his groceries, his morning milk, his newspaper, his postage stamps, and there was the use of a photocopier. There was also a hot drinks dispenser, and Mrs. Choudhury and her daughters were forever keeping the hot food cabinet filled with savoury snacks and freshly baked rolls. For Pierce it was heaven on earth. Well, almost.

The Choudhury family thought the world of their Mister Pierce, as they insisted on calling him. He was always friendly, always polite, always paid his rent and his bills, never made a fuss, never made a noise, never appeared to shop in other grocery stores, and always looked smartly dressed even when he had a day off. To them, he was the perfect tenant and loyal customer combined.

Naturally, Pierce had never mentioned his occupation and the Choudhurys had never asked. Because of the way he dressed they assumed he was something to do with the local council.

BE AWARE!
CERTAIN ILLEGAL IMMIGRANTS HAVE ARRIVED IN GATE TOWN AND COULD BE A DANGER TO THE COMMUNITY.

SHOULD YOU BECOME SUSPICIOUS OF ANYONE OR ANYTHING, TELEPHONE 00772224111 IMMEDIATELY. NO MATTER HOW TRIVIAL YOUR

SUSPICIONS MAY BE, THEY COULD BE OF VITAL IMPORTANCE TO US.

IF YOU HAVE DOUBTS, HOWEVER SMALL, DO NOT HESITATE, MAKE THAT CALL!

The dramatically written leaflets, reminiscent of WW2 warning posters, had been distributed to local traders. As Pierce left the shop one morning Mr. Choudhury had showed him his leaflet. Pierce had smiled politely, but showed little interest.

In contrast, Annette's sister Louise had shown a great deal of interest in the possibility of questionable strangers living in Gate Town. Several weeks ago she had heard the warning being broadcast on the local radio. Louise had a couple of axes to grind. One was that her sister had ignored her somewhat since she'd met the love of her life. Secondly, there was the thought of Annette's future spouse becoming joint owner of the small terraced house once her mother had passed away.

Because she and her husband were reasonably well off, Louise had no real need of a share of the house. Nor did she wish to deprive her sister of a home. But she didn't want someone dodgy getting his hands on the property. And, for all his politeness, she found David Doughty very dodgy indeed. After one or two conversations with him she came to the conclusion that he was someone without a past and without a future. So, for the sake of her sister and any future inheritance, she invited herself to tea one afternoon.

The living room took up most of the ground floor of Annette's house. And the dining table had an old-fashioned chenille tablecloth. In fact, the whole room was old-fashioned with its polished brown furniture and dated ornaments and old framed pictures that Doughty had found fascinating.

Annette had always loved the furniture and bits and pieces both as a child and as a young woman, so when her mum eventually had to downsize and move into a retirement flat, Annette had jumped at the chance of acquiring all these relics that she held dear. Luckily, Louise wanted nothing to do with what she called junk only fit for the tip.

There were times when Louise had also been puzzled by some of Doughty's strange words. They were infrequent, but on this occasion, as the three of them sat together chatting with a pot of tea and some biscuits, he uttered two of them without realising and Louise pulled him up on it.

Inwardly, Doughty cursed himself for allowing

the slip up, particularly as he had tried his hardest to keep these mistakes in check. He explained that he had once been in Kenya and these were native words. He then tried to change the subject, but Louise was not having that. She insisted on knowing why he was in that country, and did he speak the language fluently? Doughty's reply was that he was working for an English mineral mining company in Mombasa and a full knowledge of the local lingo wasn't necessary.

By the time Louise had begun to launch into even more personal questions, Annette decided she'd had enough and had politely shown her sister the front door.

When Louise had reached home that day she recalled the radio broadcast message asking for members of the public to report anything or anyone they found suspicious, no matter now insignificant they thought those suspicions might be. She opened up her computer and searched online for the words used by Doughty in both official and regional Kenyan languages, but without luck. Neither could she find a mineral mine in Mombasa itself, the nearest one being some forty miles from the city. And it was not an English owned company.

Finding the telephone number that she had

written down during the radio broadcast, Louise called the number.

Pierce arrived at the Palmers' flat to find a couple of forensic workers giving the place a thorough examination.

Bonner, wearing protective gloves, was in the kitchen. 'The woman and kid didn't leave much,' he told Pierce. 'Cupboards are almost bare. There's sod all in the freezer.' He opened the fridge door and looked inside. There was just one egg, a half bottle of milk and some rotting vegetables. He closed the fridge door. He looked at the decrepit cooker and the cheap, well-worn work surfaces. 'What a shit place this is.'

'The letting agents told me she and the kid arrived from out of nowhere in May,' said Pierce. 'Always paid her bills and the rent. In cash. But she's been a bit behind lately. They were all set to put pressure on her. Pay up or get out.'

'Did she have references?' asked Bonner.

'These agents don't bother with references. They're just glad to get someone living here.'

'I'm not surprised,' said Bonner as he walked out into the tacky hallway. He grabbed a door handle. 'So where's this fucking magical doorway that transports us to a land of enchantment?'

He opened the door. Inside was a grotty airing cupboard.

Pierce gave a humourless smile. 'Maybe you're supposed to say the magical word.'

'How about bollocks?' said Bonner as he closed the airing cupboard door.

An opaque security window, set high up in the wall, allowed some daylight into the side ward at Charnham Cross.

Eve was tidying Cara's bed as the nurse ushered the child back into the room. Nurse Claire was in her late thirties. She was a polite, friendly, noncommittal woman who was kind to Cara. 'I'll get you a drink, sweetheart,' she said as she gathered up a plastic beaker and a couple of plastic plates before walking from the room. She locked the door behind her.

'Mama, I saw a man,' said Cara. 'He's like you.'

Eve had moved to straighten her bed. 'What do you mean, he's like me?'

Cara moved to her mother. She pulled at the distinctively coloured jumpsuit. 'He wears these. Like you.'

Eve turned slowly. She stared at Cara. 'Where did you see this man?'

But Cara had lost interest. 'I don't know,' she

said as she carried the doll to her own bed.

Eve walked across the room. She took Cara gently by the shoulders and turned her so that she could look her in the eyes. 'I said, where did you see him, Cara? Tell me. It's important.'

Cara was fussing with her doll. 'He was outside,' she said.

'Did he speak to you?'

Cara shook her head. She placed the doll on her pillow.

'Well, what did he look like?'

'I forget,' said Cara. She hummed to herself as she arranged the covers around the doll.

A few days before her so-called arrest, Eve had taken Cara into town. They'd shopped for some items, but nothing expensive. From a small stationery shop she'd bought a tubular pencil box, some coloured pencils and two drawing books for Cara and a dark red plastic folder for herself.

This stupid system of exchanging complicated and cumbersome forms of currency for much-needed household items was becoming even more of a problem because the said currency was running low. Cara was always amused by the use of coins and paper money and plastic. But when Eve told her that even further back, in ancient times, people used all sorts of things for barter, including salt and livestock, the child laughed out loud.

So things were definitely bad for Eve. Six months had passed and someone should have followed. Someone who would have brought more funds. Brought more information. Brought advice. So what had gone wrong?

It was a dry day but quite windy, and, in this part of town, dust and grit from the seemingly endless procession of construction lorries seemed to fill the air. It made Cara rub at one of her eyes and complain of thirst. So they found a cheap but uncomfortable café where Eve had bought coffee and a sandwich for herself and a soft drink and a cake for Cara. She then became aware of the elderly café owner watching them curiously, as if a woman and child were a rarity in this shoddy, male dominated place.

A friendly young worker was sitting nearby with a couple of mates. He was smiling at Cara. 'Hello, little'n. What's your name?'

Cara looked up from her drink. 'I'm Cara.'

'You from round here, Cara?'

Cara shook her head and continued to rub her eye. Eve noticed that the café owner was still staring at them. She gathered her shopping together. 'Drink up, Cara. We must go.'

The young worker was persistent. 'So where you from?'

'Province seven-five.' said the child.

'Cara!' Eve spoke sharply.

One of the worker's mates had joined in. 'So where's Province Seven-five?'

'It's home,' said Cara.

Eve got quickly to her feet. 'Come on. Leave that.'

She snatched the drink from Cara then hurried the child out into the busy, noisy street. The café owner and the workers watched them go.

4

Three pneumatic drills seemed to be trying to outdo each other with their juddering, brain-numbing sounds as Jace, with the collar of her blue PVC coat turned up against the cold, walked along Ferry Lane. She was smoking a roll-up and carrying a carton of milk. The air nearby was filled with dust.

Jace was rarely seen without her blue coat. She'd bought it in a charity shop. It was very sixties and had seen better days. But she looked sexy in it and she loved it.

She passed an old weathered sign that read 'Gate Town Business Park.' Someone had aerosoled out the word 'Gate' and scrawled 'Shit' in its place. This made sense because the business park was a thing of the past and the area was now a mishmash of lorry parks, lock-ups, scrap metal yards and old buildings due for demolition. One such building was the victim of the demolition workers and their drills.

Jace stopped to look in the direction of the noise. High up, through the dusty air, she could see men in hard hats drilling at the solid upper floors of the old building. The roof had gone and so had most of the upper walls. Down below, in what would once have been a yard, was a mass of bricks, masonry, broken glass, splintered doors and busted window frames. Part of an old company sign could be seen hanging at an angle from one of the few remaining walls of the yard. If one looked hard enough one could just make out that this flaked and faded piece of advertising depicted a young and happy middle class couple pointing and smiling at a large tin of paint.

Situated in Chapel Street, just off the main shopping area of Gate Town, was a small eye care centre. Martin Pugh the optician and Sandra his assistant-cum-receptionist were the only members of staff. Business wasn't going too well for them these days. Martin blamed the two cheap and cheerful opticians in the town centre for that. But there were other reasons. There was an old-fashioned feel to Martin's establishment because, like the man himself, it was set in the past with its strict working guidelines, its one to two p.m.

daily lunch hours, and its early closing days every Wednesday.

After their trip to the shops and the grim café, Cara had kept Eve awake half the night by crying and fidgeting. Her eye was still troubling her and now the surrounding area was red from the child's constant rubbing of it. Eve had looked in the eye but could see nothing.

She and the child had not signed on at a medical centre for fear of questions. She had been warned that that was a risk she must take until others arrived to advise her. In the morning she had got Cara dressed and she and the child headed out to find a chemist shop and a pharmacist who would hopefully ask no questions. Then, with Cara still whining and complaining, they turned into Chapel Street and saw the small out-of-the-way opticians.

A bell on the door jingled as Eve and Cara entered the eye centre. Eve had told the assistant that they were in a hurry and couldn't stay long, but if some medication could be given for her daughter's eye problem it would be much appreciated. Sandra the assistant was more than helpful and ready to oblige. But Martin was lurking and wasn't going to pass up on this one. After all, eyes were his business, and he insisted on giving Cara a quick examination. Eve tried to avoid this, but by now

Cara was crying and Martin was adamant.

Sandra had kept up a cheery chat about the weather and the cost of living while Eve grew increasingly agitated with the length of time the optician was taking. When at last he and Cara emerged from the consulting room, Martin appeared to be in a state of bewilderment. But Cara had stopped crying. Still in a perplexed state, Martin told Eve that he had found a speck of grit in the pouch of the child's lower eyelid and had removed it. He then prescribed an eye bath and some hypromellose drops.

As Sandra produced the medication, Martin asked Eve if she'd be kind enough to tell him who had been her last optician and who was her GP? But Eve didn't answer. She paid for the items, took Cara by the hand and walked quickly out into the street, leaving Martin to remain staring in the direction of his departing customers.

Sandra at last saw the look on his face. 'What is it, Martin?' she had asked.

'It doesn't make sense,' he said.

'What doesn't?'

Martin moved to the door. 'Look, hold the fort for a moment, will you?'

The small bell jingled furiously as he jerked open the door.

'Please tell me, Martin. What's wrong?'

Martin stopped. He turned. He remained dumbfounded. 'By rights, that child shouldn't be able to see at all,' he said. 'Her eyes aren't real.'

Martin had hurried along Chapel Street but there was no sign of the woman. He had remembered them turning towards the high street, so he headed in that direction. Upon reaching the high street he told himself that this was crazy. And, as he weaved in and out of the passers-by, he wondered if he'd got the examination wrong, but he was sure he hadn't. He also told himself that he couldn't let this go, couldn't let the pair disappear forever. He somehow had to find out who they were, or at least where they lived.

The high street was as busy as ever with the constant movement of people and passing traffic. Martin then saw the woman and child up ahead on the other side of the street, moving away from the main shopping section. He dodged a van and a couple of cars, then almost collided with a cyclist as he crossed the street. As the passers-by began to thin out he continued to follow mother and child at a reasonable distance until they had reached the environs of Prior Street, the start of one of the most run-down areas. As vehicles continued to pass by loudly and relentlessly, the woman and child stopped at a drab looking terraced house. They climbed the front steps, unlocked and opened the front door, then entered.

When Martin Pugh returned to his eye centre he rang a couple of colleagues. He told them what he believed he'd found, but was not taken seriously. One of the colleagues even managed a joke, telling him that maybe he needed to see an optician. Then Sandra appeared at his desk with a nice cup of tea and a copy of the warning leaflet. She suggested that maybe the woman and child came from abroad. Martin immediately pooh-poohed the idea, saying that the world was not such a big place, not these days, and if such an advancement in ophthalmology had taken place we would have heard about it by now.

Sandra held out the leaflet.

'What is that?' Martin asked.

'It's a leaflet. Read it.'

Martin sighed irritably. He took the leaflet and proceeded to read it, then stopped. 'A danger to the community? How on Earth can a mother and a small child be a danger?'

Sandra moved around the desk. She leant forward and tapped a red painted fingernail on the leaflet. 'No matter how trivial your suspicions may seem to be,' she read aloud, 'they could be of vital importance to us.' She straightened up and looked directly at Martin for a moment or two. 'A child with imitation eyes, Martin? How trivial is that?'

Martin leant back in his chair. He touched his own eyes, as if unconsciously examining them.

Sandra took the leaflet from him. 'I think we'd better call them. Don't you?'

The interview room at Charnham Cross had seen better days, but it was clean and tidy, if a little bare, and had been furnished with a plain, boardroom style table and half a dozen upright chairs. There were no windows. But there was an oblong mirror, two-way of course, a camera recorder, already running, and an audio interview recorder.

Eve Palmer sat at the table. A female guard stood by the locked door.

In a narrow side room adjoining the interview room, Pierce was watching Eve through the two-way mirror. The leading forensic officer entered the side room. She carried a document case. Her name was Allie and she was a big-built woman in her late twenties who always wore tight blouses and short skirts despite her size. But she could get away with it. And she did so, whilst providing some of the most looked-forward-to, up-skirt glimpses for many of the men at Charnham Cross, plus one or two of the women.

In the interview room, Eve turned to the security officer. She spoke with an edge to her voice. 'There's nothing to drink in here.'

The guard ignored her.

Like a command, 'Did you hear me? I'd like something to drink, please.'

The guard continued to ignore her. Eve gave the woman a glare, then settled back in her chair.

Allie was still watching Eve through the mirror. 'Spiky.'

'Yeah,' said Pierce.

Allie sat down next to him. She crossed her large but shapely legs and opened the document case. She produced some paperwork and checked a list. 'Some of the woman's clothes and the child's were definitely bought locally.'

'And the rest?'

'They would have travelled back with them. As with the other two downtimers, the clothes they brought would be a mock-up of present day wear. They're a mixture of synthetic fibres. All of them known to us. They obviously made sure of that, thinking they'd give the game away too easily if they used something alien. But carbon dating may help unless they've found a way around that as well.' She continued to check her list. 'The child only had the one bagful of toys. Most have been purchased from local shops.'

'And the ID?'

'Still being checked. They had full birth certificates and passports, similar to the ones the others were carrying. They have to be counterfeit.'

'But brilliantly done?'

'Yes. Just like the money. That must be as perfect as you can get. And the law tells us that it's up to individuals to check if they've been given a duff banknote. But how many people do that? Most counterfeits get discovered via the banking system. Then they record 'em and take 'em out of circulation. So, if there are no names or descriptions, then no arrest.'

Allie proceeded to gather up her paperwork. 'Anyhow, my team's made a thorough examination of the flat they were living in, down to the last manky bit of floor covering. So, the answer to the question we've all been asking is....'

'There's still nothing to show how they got here.'

'Right.' Allie reached for her briefcase. She put her paperwork back inside it.

'Did you hear about the kid's eyes?' asked

Pierce.

'Yes,' said Allie.

'It's crazy. It's like she's wearing glasses on the inside.'

Pierce looked up as, through the two-way mirror, the guard could be seen unlocking the interview room door.

Mrs. O'Day and Bonner entered the interview room. Bonner carried some bottled water and plastic cups. He placed them on the table as the security officer left the room. Mrs. O'Day sat down to face Eve as Bonner took his seat and proceeded to start the interview recorder. Eve watched this with just the faintest trace of amusement.

Mrs. O'Day was looking carefully at Eve. 'If I had the means to travel back a hundred or so years in time, I'd need a good excuse for doing so,' she said. 'What's your excuse?'

Eve said nothing. She indicated the bottle of water. 'May I?'

Bonner reached for the bottle. He poured Eve a cup of water.

'You see, I'm a warm bodied person who can't handle too much cold,' continued Mrs. O'Day. 'I like my comforts. Always have. And if I went back to, say, the early twentieth century, I wouldn't have many of those. Unless I was well-off. Or privileged. I certainly wouldn't have the career I have now. Or a vote. So I'd probably be cold, poor, misrepresented and bloody miserable.'

Eve said nothing. She sipped at her water.

'Of course, if I travelled the same distance into the future I'd learn things. Wouldn't I?'

Once more, Eve said nothing.

'And probably the first question on my list would be how people like you managed to travel back. So tell us. How did you get here?'

'It's difficult to explain.'

'I bet it is. But try your best, why don't you? Were you shot out of a fucking cannon? Did you get into a lift and press the wrong button?'

'I don't know. I don't remember.'

'What do you mean, you don't remember? How could you *not* remember?'

'I was asleep.'

'We've heard that one before,' said Bonner quietly.

Upon hearing this, Eve became a little wary. But she didn't show it. She simply glanced at Bonner, then back.

'So are you telling us this was done without your knowledge?' asked Mrs. O'Day.

'Of course not.'

'Then what do you mean?'

'My child and I were anaesthetized.'

'By who?'

'By the people who sent us here.'

'Why would they send you here?'

'Because we agreed to come.'

'And who are these people? Are they part of the government?'

'We don't have a government. Not in the way that you would understand.'

Mrs. O'Day raised her voice. 'Well I don't give a fuck what you condescendingly think we should understand. You're in our time now. Not yours. You're here with the poor old knuckle-draggers. Have you got that?'

Eve nodded, reluctantly.

'So it was a private organization that sent you?'

'Yes.'

'And does this organization have a name?'

Eve reckoned she had nothing to lose by revealing the name. 'It's called Timelight.'

'And did you pay for this privilege?'

'No. I volunteered.'

'So why are you here? Are you running away from something?'

Eve shook her head.

'Or someone?'

'No.'

'In your own time period, do you have a career?

'Yes.'

'What is it?'

'I'm a lecturer. In history.'

Mrs. O'Day glanced at Bonner. He gave a little disbelieving roll of the eyes.

'Are you really trying to tell us you're on some kind of field trip?' said Mrs. O'Day.

Eve hesitated for just a moment. 'Yes. I am.'

'Well, from my experience, people on field trips have a look around, have a bit of lunch, maybe chat each other up, make a few notes, take a few samples, trample to death a bit of wildlife, then get back on the bus and go home.'

Eve said nothing.

'Is there a way back for you?'

'No. Not without help.'

'Bit of a suicide trip then, isn't it?'

Once more, Eve said nothing.

'And with a child in tow.'

Again, Eve said nothing.

'Is that why you gave yourself up?'

Yet again, Eve said nothing.

'What about the child's father?'

'He's no longer with us.'

'Why?'

'We had no further use for each other.'

'And are there others here from your time period?'

'I wouldn't know,' said Eve.

Mrs. O'Day looked at Bonner. She then got up from her chair. She took a packet of cigarettes and a lighter from her pocket. She lit the cigarette. She took a little walk around the room. She glanced at the two-way mirror as she passed it.

In the side room, Pierce and Allie continued to watch the events.

'Do we believe the lady?' asked Allie.

'Haven't made my mind up yet,' said Pierce.

In the interview room Bonner adjusted his chair. He looked at Eve. 'Our medical officer tells us that you and your daughter are in excellent health.'

'I could have told him that,' said Eve.

'But he was particularly interested in your little girl's vision.'

As soon as Eve and Cara had been brought to Charnham Cross the M.O. had made a more thorough examination of the child. He had also sent for a military colleague, an ophthalmic surgeon. Their findings seemed to suggest that there was no evidence of stem cell self-renewal and that all three main layers of Cara's eyes, as well as the middle layers, were artificial. So, too, were the retinas and all small muscles, glands and nerves.

'Can you tell us about her eyes?' asked Bonner.

'She was partially blind when she was born,' said Eve. 'As a disadvantaged child she was given nothing more than replacement surgery. It's commonplace.'

'Not to us.'

Eve ignored the remark. She turned to Mrs. O'Day. 'My daughter has very little to occupy her mind in this place. Could she at least have her drawing books and pencils? They *are* hers.'

Mrs. O'Day did not reply. She continued her walk around the room.

Bonner took a plain white envelope from his inside pocket. 'So you say you know nothing about others like you,' he said as he opened the envelope. He produced a photograph of Doughty dressed in his wedding day suit. He placed the photograph on the table top in front of Eve. 'Well, let's see. Do you know this man?'

Eve glanced at the photograph. 'No.'

'Are you sure? Only he happens to be a fellow traveller of yours.'

Eve was taken aback by this. She wondered if it was a trick, just a guess on their part. After all, how could they possibly know she was expecting someone? Someone she would have recognised. Because of this, she hesitated yet again. Mrs. O'Day did not miss the hesitation.

'He calls himself David Doughty,' said Bonner. 'And for someone who's travelled back all this way in time, he's also enjoying good health.'

'I'm glad to hear it,' said Eve.

'I think it's time we spelled things out for you, Mrs. Palmer, or whatever your name is,' said Mrs. O'Day as she used her shoe to stub her cigarette out on the floor. She then sat back down at the table. 'You see, we don't really care about the hardships your little joyride may have caused you. It's not for us to worry about. At the same time we do represent members of a small, but powerful higher authority. And we've been instructed to prepare the way, because, right now, that higher authority is not quite sure what to do with people like you.'

Eve took another sip of her water as Mrs. O'Day continued. 'But there are a few things that the aforementioned have definitely made up their minds about. To start with, they don't want the general public to know anything about you. Nor the press. Nor the TV companies. Nor the sci-fi nuts and pacifists and do-gooders. Nor the church. Especially not the church, because that would mean a load of clap-happy loons hoping to get an update on the existence of God.' She stopped for a moment. She looked directly at Eve. 'Is there one?'

PJ Hammond

Eve had just the tiniest of smiles. 'We're still looking,' she replied.

'Oh, good,' said Mrs. O'Day, disgruntled by both the reply and the smile. 'I'm glad we're beginning to understand each other. Because the last thing those in charge need is you and your kind telling us just how advanced and clever you are. Well, not for the moment, anyway. And although we here in this room would love to know how you can predict things by giving us crafty little bits of information on, say, when our current prime minister or our monarch will die. Or how they will meet their deaths. Or what unavoidable disasters are about to befall us in the next hundred years or so. Yes, we'd really enjoy that. We'd pull up our chairs and listen intently to every last word. However, in the interest of national security we've been ordered not to ask you those questions. You see, we're just the workers who sweat and toil away at the coal face. But in due course those questions will indeed be asked of you, and answers dragged from you, by others who may not be quite as polite and patient as people like me.'

Bonner had a smile to himself as Mrs. O'Day lit another cigarette.

'Because,' Mrs. O'Day continued, 'and I hope to fuck you appreciate this, that higher authority of

64

ours does not want this knowledge of yours getting into the wrong hands. That's the big one. The big scare. The big fear. You see, we've no idea how civilized and worldly wise you are, along there in the future. But here and now, in this sometimes pretty but mostly shitty time of ours, there are too many murdering maniacs. Too many crazy zealots. And, left to your own devices, your kind would be far too easy and far too useful as targets for criminals, terrorists, regimes that sponsor terrorism, or even individual nutjobs with grievances and murder in mind. This means that you and others like you are a threat to us, Mrs. Palmer. A very serious one. And that includes your child. So you could say that in a way this higher authority of ours is in fear of you.'

Mrs. O'Day shoved her chair back once more. She got up from the table.

'So what happens to us?' asked Eve.

Mrs. O'Day didn't answer. Eve watched her as she walked to the door and waited there.

'Joseph Valentine,' said Bonner.

Eve turned her head to look at him. 'What?'

'Do you know the name?'

Eve gave a weary and impatient sigh. 'No.'

'Only he arrived here in the same way as you and your daughter and Mr. Doughty.'

Eve was aware of Mrs. O'Day watching her

and probably waiting for a response. Believing it to be another trick, she said nothing.

'It's a pity you couldn't have all travelled back here together,' said Mrs. O'Day as she puffed on her cigarette. 'You could have had a bit of a knees-up on the way.'

'Our guess is that Joseph Valentine would have been in his late twenties,' Bonner continued. 'But maybe his health wasn't that good. Because he was found dead on arrival.'

Some quick thoughts went through Eve's mind. One or two people who could have come here to help her would have been around about that age. And, of course, they wouldn't be using their own names. She wondered, should she ask more, or is that what these two interrogators were waiting for her to do? She decided to say nothing.

'Could the journey back have killed him?' asked Bonner. 'Were you warned about such possibilities?'

'No,' said Eve, still trying to avoid a trap.

'Could others have died?'

'How would I know?'

Bonner kept up the pressure. 'Or maybe they could have got lost in the ether somewhere. Sort of between worlds, maybe?'

On hearing this, Eve gave an inward shiver.

'Sorry you can't help us, Mrs. Palmer. I mean, we don't have the answers, do we?' said Bonner. 'Not back here where we belong. We're far too dumb.' He switched off the interview recorder and rose from his chair.

'You still haven't said what happens to us,' said Eve. 'To me and my child.'

'I'm afraid you'll have to remain in a secure unit,' said Mrs. O'Day.

'In this place? It's not fit to live in.'

'It's all we've got.'

'So how long are we going to be here?'

'Possibly forever.'

Eve stared in dismay as Bonner knocked hard upon the door, which was then unlocked and opened by the guard.

Mrs. O'Day and Bonner were joined by Pierce as they made their way back towards the administration block.

'Sometime, somehow, we'll need to talk to the child,' said Mrs. O'Day. 'Alone.'

'Tricky,' said Pierce.

'Yes,' agreed Mrs. O'Day. 'So let's begin by making life a little easier for her.' She turned to Bonner. 'Her books and pencils, have they been cleared?'

'I think so. Yes.'

'Then let her have them.'

They reached the end of the secure area. Mrs. O'Day stopped and looked from a window. She watched David Doughty as he took his exercise walk in the fenced-off compound. 'By the way, the poor bride is upset.'

'Understandable,' said Bonner.

'She even tried to write a letter of complaint to the local newspaper.' Mrs. O'Day turned from the window. 'I know there's a Defence Notice in place, but I don't want her getting any other ideas. Visit her tomorrow, will you? See if you can shut her up.'

Nurse Claire walked Cara through the deserted main ward of the old hospital. They were met by Eve who was being escorted to the door of the side ward by the guard. Cara called out to Eve and the nurse allowed the child to run to her mother. She lifted Cara up into her arms and held her tightly. Cara saw tears in Eve's eyes and on her cheeks. She reached out with a tiny finger and touched the tears.

'What's wrong, Mama?'

'Nothing, love,' said Eve, holding Cara even more closely to her. 'Everything's fine.'

During their stay in the Gate Town flat, Eve

and Cara had taken several bus rides. There wasn't much to see in the town, but Cara liked to ride on what she called the 'funny old buses'. Occasionally they would visit the town cemetery. It was a vast sprawl of a place, close to the ring road, and over-populated with graves. Cara hated it there, but she was forced to tag along with her mother while she walked the many narrow grass paths between gravestones.

Bonner followed Allie to a forbidding looking building in the old parade ground at Charnham Cross. It had been the camp's solitary confinement blockhouse in days gone by, with cells below ground and an exercise and work unit in the two floors above. But during the Second World War those two floors had been adapted to accommodate a double gallows. This execution suite, as it was politely called, was used for the judicial hangings of serving soldiers who had committed murder or rape.

Allie and Bonner descended concrete steps that led to the building's basement.

While bride and groom and wedding guests were entering the registry office on that fateful wedding day, Bonner and Pierce had already gained access to Annette's house. They quickly and methodically removed all of David Doughty's personal effects before making their way to wait and to greet the newlyweds.

Bonner and Pierce had later spoken with Doughty about the faked items that had travelled back with him and asked why he had not brought something more advantageous with him from the future. Doughty had told them that it wasn't allowed on ethical grounds and would also compromise the rule of not revealing oneself. This backed up the results of the search of Annette's property and the flat where Eve and her daughter had been living.

Whilst appreciating the downtiming rules, Bonner was surprised that no-one would dare break them. 'You'd think they would have tried something, wouldn't you?' he had said to Pierce over a lunchtime drink. 'Nothing big. Nothing stupid. Just something small and handy, something that could make you a few bob. Or open a few doors.'

Allie led the way along an underground corridor, past long disused cells, until they reached what was now the protective storage unit, where they were obliged to sign themselves in.

After a thorough examination, Eve and Cara's possessions had all been logged, bagged up and buried away inside the unit along with David Doughty's personal belongings and the very few items found on the body of the dead downtimer.

The property officer in charge unlocked and entered a rear room, where he could be heard clattering around opening metal cupboards. Bonner shivered. He rubbed his hands together. 'Bloody cold down here.'

Allie smiled at him. 'I don't feel the cold.'

'Lucky you.' He watched her as she wandered across the room to study some information posters attached to the wall. He idly and innocently wondered what it would be like to have those fine big thighs wrapped around his neck. 'You saw the interview?'

'Yes, Sir.'

'What did you think of our latest arrival?'

'I'm not sure of her.'

'In what way?'

'I don't know, but I'm just not sure.' She turned from the posters. 'Just a feeling, that's all.'

The property officer reappeared. He carried a clear polythene bag that contained Cara's drawing books and the tubular case of coloured pencils. Bonner reached for the bag. He peered through the polythene. 'All bought locally, you say?'

'That's right,' said Allie.

Bonner took a pen from his pocket. He signed the booking-out form.

Mrs. O'Day and Bonner sat together in the consulting room of the old hospital wing. Mrs. O'Day smoked a fag and drank coffee from a paper cup as they watched Eve and Cara on yet another surveillance screen.

Both mother and child could be seen eating a meal in the side ward as the door was unlocked and nurse Claire entered. She carried the drawing books and pencil case. Cara left her meal and scrambled down from her chair to get the items. Claire smiled at her, then left the room and locked it as usual. Cara was delighted. She carried the drawing books and pencil case to her bed. She opened one of the books. She unzipped the pencil case and checked her coloured pencils. She then began to do some drawing.

'Good,' said Mrs. O'Day. 'That'll keep her happy.'

Bonner was not that impressed. 'A couple of books and a few pencils?'

'Oh, I haven't finished yet.'

Mrs. O'Day reached out and switched off the

screen. She then sat in thought for a moment before saying, 'So some poxy outfit in the future has sent this woman back so that she can live in a crap flat and buy her kid a few toys.'

'That's her version,' said Bonner. 'But who are we supposed to believe? We can't exactly ring the outfit up and tell 'em they can't fuck around with time, now can we? And that's the problem. We have no real control over things.'

'Of course we don't have any proper control. Don't you think I'm aware of that? We just do the best we fucking can. We check these people out, then we lock them up. And we keep on doing that until we know more.' Mrs. O'Day finished her coffee, dumped the butt of her cigarette into the coffee dregs, then got up from her chair. 'Trouble is, we don't know what else the bastards can send back, either by accident or design. We could get some bad shit.'

Bonner nodded in agreement. 'Do you remember that old paradox joke about going back to the past and bumping off your great, great granddad?'

'Remind me,' said Mrs. O'Day as she moved to the door.

'You disappear up your own ancestry.'
Mrs. O'Day laughed out loud. She had the laugh of a pissed-up squaddie on a night out.

5

Jace lived in a small two bedroom flat. It was situated up a flight of narrow stairs, above a car rental office in Ferry Lane. But no-one was ever seen in the office. And there were never any cars. Bonner reckoned it was probably a front for some kind of dodgy business.

Jace liked cloth, and she was forever searching for items in Gate Town's charity shops. The main bedroom, her own private room, was filled with old neck scarves, head scarves, big coloured hankies, sashes, ribbons, old lengths of discarded curtain and dress materials, scraps of lace, and small commemorative flags and banners. But there was never anything too kitsch or too jokey. That wasn't her style. The items had been draped, or rather deliberately flung, with great care and precision, pattern upon pattern, colour upon colour, odd size upon odd length, layer after layer, so that very little of the actual walls could be seen. When the sun shone through the windows it gave a silky, kaleidoscopic effect. Sounds were somehow woolly and muffled in this room. And Jace liked that.

In complete contrast, the smaller of the two bedrooms contained just a bed and a chair and no decorations of any kind, apart from a couple of sixties pin-up posters. This was Jace's business room for punters.

Bonner had dropped by that evening on his way home. He had brought takeaway spicy chicken, fried rice and bean sprouts. He and Jace had eaten these before making love in the main bedroom. They now lay there amid the draped and hushed softness of the room.

'Funny name you got. Solomon,' said Jace as she made herself a roll-up from an old tobacco tin. She had decorated the small tin herself with tiny beads and sequins stuck on with Evo Stik. 'So-lo-mon,' she intoned the name in a solemn voice. 'I seem to remember it being in some sort of kid's rhyme.'

'Yeah, said Bonner, 'Solomon Grundy, got pissed on Monday...'

'That's not it...'

'Felt sick as a fart on Tuesday. Couldn't get it up on Wednesday.'

Jace laughed. 'Then what?'

'I dunno.'

'So why were you called that?'

'My dad was a salt-of-the-earth, C of E, shoe repairer. Didn't have much money but he had his own little shop. Wanted me to be named Colin. But me mum was seriously Jewish. And she always had the last word.'

He settled back in the bed as Jace lit her roll-up. He had first met her when she was a witness to an assault on another working girl. He had been the investigating officer at the time. He'd had a drink with her in the Gantry after a long, hard day, and that was that. And it didn't matter to him that Jace could look seventeen. That was just coincidental. She could have looked forty-seven for all he cared. He liked her for what she was. Just being Jace. She never had a bad word to say about anyone. Jace couldn't do snide if she tried.

But it was Jace's history of self harm that sometimes worried Bonner. She had told him that she was over it, and, so far, he was prepared to believe her. He remembered when he once heard that she'd cut her wrists in a back room at a party, but was helped in time by friends.

'Don't know why I did it,' she had told him after the event. 'I just get in a funny mood and it takes over.' She'd had difficulty describing the mood to him, explaining that it wasn't sadness or depression that brought it on. But some small thing might worry her and then there would come this deadness. Just a deadness.

And now, as they lay together in this almost noiseless cocoon of a room, he recalled another part of her history that she had once revealed to him after a drink or two. It was how, as a little girl, she would hide at night from her father and her uncle. She would try to find a safe place under coats in the hallway, or under draped tablecloths, or towels in the airing cupboard. But they would always search for her. And find her.

Bonner was aware that child abuse was a characteristic of adolescent prostitution and that it could result in runaway behaviour in later life. Or, maybe in Jace's case, hideaway behaviour. At the same time there was still this crazy association with danger.

'Why don't you just give up the game?' he had suggested, following that conversation.

'I will one day,' she had promised.

Bonner lay there in thought for a while longer.

'Tell me something, Jace. What would you do if

you could go back in time? Travel back.'

'To where?'

'I don't know. Victorian times?'

Jace puffed on her roll-up. 'Depends what their bus services were like. I depend on buses.'

'Or even further back. Say, the Early Middle Ages.'

'The what?'

'You could take a plastic clothes peg with you. Or a safety pin.'

'Why?'

'You could invent them. Then again, that's probably not a good idea. You'd get burnt as a witch.'

'I'd rather kill meself.'

Bonner smiled

'Remember when I told the girls I'd swallowed some Parazone bleach?'

'Nobody thought that was funny.'

'I did. I was just winding 'em up. For a laugh. I mean, as if I'd do that!'

'As if!' said Bonner as he eased himself up from the pillows.

'What is it they call them suicide risks?' asked Jace. 'You told me once.'

'Vulnerables.'

'Oh, yeah.' Jace thought about this. 'I like

that word.' Once more she intoned the word, 'Vul-ner-ables.'

She reached for an ashtray as Bonner pulled back the covers. He sat on the edge of the bed.

'So why were you talking about going back in time?'

'I was just being stupid.'

'Yeah, you were. Because no-one can do that.' Jace knocked ash into the ashtray. 'We're here because this is where we've been put. No-one can change that.'

Bonner said nothing. He reached for his clothes.

Lesley was sitting at the kitchen table when Bonner arrived home. She was busy reading a brochure and making notes. He told her he wasn't hungry because he had been working late and had therefore grabbed a takeaway meal with his colleagues. But Lesley wasn't really listening. She was preoccupied. She held up the brochure and proudly announced that she was about to join the local W.I.

It was a fresh, cold morning, and at eight-fifteen Pierce was in the Choudhury corner shop fixing himself a coffee and choosing something from the hot snack cabinet. Bonner entered the shop. He joined the small queue of manual workers and bought himself a newspaper. He then moved to the snack cabinet. He looked disdainfully at Pierce's breakfast.

'Onion bhajis at this hour of the day? No wonder you live on your own.'

Pierce ignored the remark. He walked to the counter and paid Choudhury daughter number three for the items. He then nibbled at one of the bhajis and waved to Mrs. Choudhury as he followed Bonner to the door. She smiled and waved back at him.

On their way from south Gate Town to the overpass, Bonner and Pierce drove along Ferry Lane in Bonner's hatchback. The shrill clatter of the pneumatic drills could be heard as they passed the demolition area and the faded sign with its happy, suburban looking couple admiring their king-sized tin of paint.

Back in the nineteen-fifties and sixties, when Gate Town wasn't such a shit town, there were many small and medium-sized businesses doing quite well for themselves. One of these was a well-established paint manufacturing company called Dunstall & Sons. It was situated in Ferry Lane and had a workforce of seventy-six. It was considered to be an ideal firm to work for.

Dunstall & Sons was owned and run by three brothers known as Mr. Edward, Mr. Michael and Mr. Stanley. They were fair minded men and well respected, if perhaps just a tad old fashioned. And, although they insisted upon a class divide in the works canteen, with Formica topped tables in one section for the manual workers, and tablecloths in the smaller, screened-off section used by the office and managerial staff, no-one grumbled or thought militant thoughts, because the three brothers cared about their employees. If anyone had a grievance they would listen. If anyone happened to be sick for a long period they could be happy in the knowledge that their job would be waiting for them when they eventually returned to work.

Mr. Edward and Mr. Stanley were in their late fifties and were confirmed bachelors. Mr. Michael, who was the youngest by several years, was once married for a brief period until his wife ran off with a rep from a firm of wallpaper suppliers. It had been Mr. Michael's one and only serious relationship and losing her had broken his heart. But from that day onwards he had channelled all his leftover love and devotion into the company, its loyal customers and its trusted staff. So it was understandable that quite a few equally devoted

employees imagined that all those at Dunstall &
Sons were part of one big happy family under the
leadership and guidance of the three brothers.

Appreciative of this company loyalty, all three
bosses faithfully maintained and thoroughly
enjoyed organising the company's two annual
social events.

One event was a sit-down meal held each year
just before the Christmas holiday. On this occasion
there was no class divide, and all staff members
sat together on long rows of trestle-tables covered
with white tablecloths. The staff could invite their
immediate family members to this do, and there
would be collection boxes for one or two local
charities.

The get-together always began with a speech
from either Mr. Edward, Mr. Michael or Mr. Stanley,
followed by the meal itself. After that the so-called
fun began with various turns given by employees
who were in no doubt that they had a gift for
entertainment. Unfortunately, it was usually the
same turns each year. But no-one really minded.
The warehouse foreman always did his Stanley
Holloway impressions. Rob, the head colour-tinter,
played the acoustic guitar reasonably well, but
sang badly. There was the usual amateur juggler
from sales. And the same four ladies from the paint

production line, plus two from the works canteen, conducted their well-known sing-alongs, which incorporated a lethal looking high-kick dance routine.

The second social event always took place in early August. For those who wished to go, it was a one-day there-and-back trip to the coast in a small convoy of two coaches. No family members were included on this treat because of the cost and the seating availability. Each year the destination was the same, dear old Folkstone, rain or shine, because a half-cousin of the Dunstalls owned a holiday camp and entertainments centre quite close to the sea. And it was less than a hundred miles from Gate Town.

Annette Smith was definitely not happy to have Bonner and Pierce knocking at her front door. But they seemed friendlier this time, apologetic even. And she was desperate for news. So she let them into the house.

'I hope you've got something good to tell me,' she said as they entered the living room. 'Because I've not heard a word from David. He hasn't written to me. Is he allowed to? Only I'm still waiting.' She looked carefully at Bonner and Pierce. 'How is he?'

'He was in good health when we last saw him,'

said Bonner.

This caused a flicker of worry for Annette. 'What do you mean, when you last saw him?'

'He's been transferred to a more appropriate location.'

'Does that mean I can visit him? I hope so, because I think I have every right to see him. And I still don't know what he's supposed to have done wrong. No-one tells me anything.'

Pierce gave her a grave, but understanding smile. It was the smile of a courteous undertaker. 'May we sit down, Mrs. Doughty?'

'Oh. Yes. Sorry.' She indicated the dining table and chairs.

Pierce nodded a thank you. He and Bonner sat down at the chenille covered table. Annette watched them carefully once more before sitting down with them.

Bonner looked around him at the array of old ornaments and pictures before turning his attention to Annette. 'We've heard you've been writing to the local newspaper,' he said.

Annette nodded. 'Yes. Just the one letter. But it wasn't published. Obviously my problem isn't interesting enough, despite the fact that my husband has been taken from me and I've been given no information whatsoever.'

'That's why we're here,' said Bonner. 'To give you some answers. To put your mind at rest.'

Annette still wasn't that sure of them, but she felt some relief. 'Thank you,' she said and waited. But Bonner and Pierce simply sat and looked at her. Pierce gave another of his solemn, reassuring smiles.

'Well? Is he... was he a criminal?' Annette asked. 'Or someone on the run from something? I had this idea that perhaps he was a fugitive of some sort. And I was... well, I was hoping that really he was innocent, and there was some sort of misunderstanding.'

Pierce shifted gently into 'Immigration Control' mode. 'Do you know where he was living before he came here?'

'No, not really,' said Annette. 'He said he'd been working abroad for many years, in Africa and places like that.'

'Do you happen to know how he arrived here? In Gate Town?'

Annette shook her head.

'Or his means of getting here?'

'He's never said.'

'But surely you needed to know more about the man you were about to marry?'

'No. He told me a little and I felt I knew enough.

Then again, I suppose- well, I suppose I didn't want to hear…'

'Anything bad.'

Annette considered this for a moment, then nodded. 'Yes. My erm- my sister asked him questions. But then she's that sort of person.'

'What kind of questions?'

'Personal ones. I didn't like that.'

'Well, did he ever tell you why he came here in the first place?'

'No. But I've a feeling he'd been living in a part of the world that wasn't very nice. Like a desert or something.'

'Why do you think that?'

'Well, he liked to go to Providence Park almost every day. Not that it's much of a park. And… and garden centres. He'd buy me plants and things.' She indicated the outside of the window. 'Look what he's made of my back yard.'

Bonner got up from his chair and moved to the window. He looked out. The small area of yard had been neatly arranged with glazed earthenware pots and troughs and hanging baskets. Many of them were filled with evergreen plants.

'And he really admired the trees in the park. I mean, they're just trees, but he loved them, and the soil, and anything growing.' Annette remembered, with warmth. 'It's funny. Sometimes he seemed like a child let loose.'

'Did he like to visit any other places?' asked Pierce.

Annette thought about this. 'Sometimes he liked to go to the Connaught.'

Upon hearing this, Bonner turned from the window. 'The cemetery?'

'Yes. God knows why. There's not much to see there, except graves. It's got a few trees, I suppose. And flowers. Cut flowers on some of the graves all year round.' She stopped. She was losing patience. 'Will you please tell me what's happened?'

Bonner decided it was time to up the lying. He moved back to the table and sat down. 'Sorry, Mrs. Doughty, but it's not good news. The person you went through a form of marriage with, *is* a criminal.'

Annette stared at him. 'Went through a form of…' she began, then stopped, fearing the worst.

Pierce joined in with the deceit. He was even more plausible than Bonner. 'The man who calls himself David Doughty is also an illegal immigrant. Been resident in Europe for many years. In Poland mainly. Although he's moved around a lot. And he's wanted in several countries for various crimes, including theft and embezzlement.'

Annette looked stunned and bewildered. The colour had left her face. She pleaded with Bonner and Pierce as she got up from the table. 'Then at least take me to him. At least let me see him. Where is he?'

'He's been deported,' said Pierce. 'He's back in Europe.'

Annette was even more bewildered. 'You mean you forced him to go?'

'No. He was given the option of standing trial in this country or returning to Europe. He chose to return.'

'Well, surely he must have asked about me? Or left some sort of message?' She raised her voice. 'Just tell me, will you? He must have said something. Did he leave a message?'

Pierce hesitated for effect. He then shook his head. Annette now looked unsteady on her feet. She stumbled back down into her chair. Bonner put out a hand to assist her, but she shrugged him off.

'When… when you said a form of marriage, what …what did you mean?'

Bonner glanced at Pierce. The look suggested, 'Maybe she's had enough'. But Pierce's face remained impassive. 'Your so-called husband is already married,' he said.

Bonner saw Annette's body shiver. He knew

that she felt this was coming. Then Pierce proceeded to deliver the final phoney 'shut her up for good lines' just as Mrs. O'Day would have wanted them.

'He has a wife and two children in Poland.'

Annette began to cry.

But Pierce hadn't quite finished. 'We're sorry you've been taken in by him. Obviously your sister wasn't. That's why she rang us.'

After all these weeks of waiting, Annette broke at last. She gave a loud and terrible cry. A cry of pain. An animal cry. A cry of hurt and anger and anguish. During his years in the force, Bonner had heard too many cries such as this. And, right now, he never wanted to hear another one again.

Bonner took a small voice recorder from his pocket as he and Pierce walked from the house. He switched off the recorder.

'Are we bastards or are we bastards?' he asked.

'Not our problem,' said Pierce.

6

By December there were no further reports of downtimers living or arriving in the Gate Town area, although Mrs. O'Day and her team continued to listen out and wait.

In the meantime, life in Gate Town had trundled along in its own sweet way.

In the Rathbone area a fifteen year old girl, with family problems, had been missing from home for two days.

In a house not far from the Choudhurys' shop, a pensioner had convinced himself that his elderly wife had been unfaithful and had strangled her before making a messy job of hanging himself from the staircase. Pierce saw the couple's photographs on the front page of the local paper while he was buying groceries in the shop. Mr. Choudhury, a devout Muslim, said that there had to be some mistake because the dead woman had facial hair and was the ugliest creature in Christendom.

Jace had woken one morning to find a brown official envelope, addressed to Ms Jessica Anne Cassidy, on her doormat. The authoritative look of the document, worried her slightly, so she left it unopened and shoved it in a drawer for the time being.

During his incarceration at Charnham Cross, David Doughty had written several letters to Annette. Although he had been told that the letters would be posted to his wife, he had never once received a reply. To take his mind off things, he had asked if he could do some gardening work and was allowed to tidy up the overgrown borders of the compound and one or two other safe sites. He was given the use of a wheelbarrow, a spade, a rake and a broom. But to avoid the possibility of self-harm he had only been issued with a small hand-fork. Secateurs were available if needed, but could only be used by the accompanying guard.

The already badly fucked-up road widening traffic system was now in complete and utter chaos due to the collapse of a mains water supply. For almost three days, pissed-off and angry drivers had no direct access to or from the north of the town but had to rely on maddening and complicated diversions.

The body of the missing girl was found in a lane by the Connaught cemetery. She had been brutally raped and strangled. Officers from the divisional police squad were dealing.

Lesley Bonner had paid her membership fee and had been accepted by the local W.I. She went to her first meeting in the old scouts' hall in Rathbone Road and found that due to a lack of interest from those living in the area she was the youngest one there.

A young man, wearing expensive sun glasses as a means of disguise, and brandishing a length of piping, had burst into the Chain Lane betting shop and demanded money. But Mrs. Pomfret, the manageress, who could have dummied for a Sumo wrestler, was having none of it. She came from behind her security screen, wrenched the piece of piping from the would-be robber and beat the shit out of him. She also managed to smash the young thief's shades, tear his jacket from his back and rip away most of his Chinos. In the process his own cash, made up of some coins and a couple of ten pound notes, fell to the floor, along with his fags and a pricey looking lighter. He staggered from the premises with a heavy nose bleed, clutching what was left of his trousers and was last seen limping away. Mrs. Pomfret threw the piece of piping out into the street, calmly gathered up the scattered money, lighter and fags and went back to work.

During a quiet evening session at the Gantry, Jace had blamed the traffic shambles for affecting trade for her and some of the other girls, which it hadn't. Bonner had popped in for a drink and tried to explain to her that geographically her complaint made no sense. But he was wasting his time. Jace had swanned into the pub in her usual manner, dressed as always in her old blue PVC coat, and with a new girl in tow. Bonner was convinced that the girl was too young to be served alcohol, but Clumpy Ron had no objections and poured the 'baby-pro' a half of lager.

Jace took Bonner to one side and told him that the girl, named Rosa, was eighteen but could look and be 'school' whenever the punters wanted.

Bonner looked at the girl and felt sad. She was a plain kid, and in a crazy, unfair way it was probably only those lost little girl looks that enabled her to get the work. Bonner also felt despair and disgust knowing that there were sick bastards who needed this and were prepared to pay for it. And kill for it, he reminded himself, following the recent murder of the local schoolgirl. And he was glad that he and Lesley had never had a child, especially a daughter.

In the Cat in the Cradle pub in East Street, an odd novelty act was taking place. It could be a rowdy pub, where karaoke singers and the occasional would-be stand-up comedian could be given a bad time by hecklers. But this man had captivated his audience by stepping up on to the rostrum to do a short, impromptu magic act. He was a tall, lean, muscular man, probably in his early to mid-forties, and the act had only lasted for about four minutes, but it had managed to quieten the usually noisy crowd during that short time. The man had invited one of the young barmaids to sit in an upright chair. Then, with a very fast flick of his hand, he had produced what looked like a cluster of brilliantly coloured lights from his pocket and succeeded in raising both girl and chair four feet into the air with no apparent effort.

When the landlord and some customers tried to buy the man a drink, they found he had left. No-one knew his name and no-one had seen him before.

Unknown to anyone, this stranger and 'one-off performer' of the Gate Town night life, what there was of it, had given himself the name Shad.

Bonner had gone out for a drink that evening because Lesley was cheerfully making what seemed like an entire vat of marmalade and the kitchen stank and was full of steam. And Bonner hated marmalade. When he arrived home he found that Lesley had gone to bed but the place still reeked of marmalade. And there were now jars and jars of the poxy nondescript stuff in the kitchen, each one waiting to be labelled and dated.

That same evening, in the side ward of the old Charnham Cross hospital, Eve was filling the wash basin. She turned off the tap then undid the top of her jumpsuit before slipping it from her shoulders to her waist. Although for security reasons the ward was open-plan, with the loo, shower and wash basin in the alcove, Eve had discovered that for the sake of modesty she could ease to one side of the alcove and be out of range of the surveillance camera high up near the ceiling.

As Eve proceeded to wash and dry herself she heard a clattering sound. She turned to look. Earlier, Cara had gone to sleep with one of her drawing books and the opened pencil case on top of the bed covers. Now she had turned over in her sleep and the pencil case had fallen to the floor, spilling out most of the pencils.

Eve was alarmed, but, aware of the camera, acted as if nothing untoward had happened. She draped the towel around her shoulders before casually moving to gather up the pencils. She put them back in the case and zipped it up with a feeling of great relief.

It was two in the morning and a couple of young late night clubbers walked together along Ferry Lane. The girl had taken off her high heeled shoes and was carrying them. Her skirt was far too short for such a cold night. The lad had his arm around her in an attempt to keep her warm. They walked on, laughing together and chattering and shivering as they passed by the fenced off demolition site with its hazard warning signs and the jagged silhouette of what was once the old paint factory.

7

On August the fifth, nineteen-sixty-one, Mr. Edward, Mr. Michael and Mr. Stanley, along with sixty-eight members of staff, had gathered in the yard of Dunstall & Sons for the grand August outing. It was early on a Saturday morning and two motor coaches were parked up and waiting.

The brother-in-law of Mr. Selby from packing had generously agreed to drop by and film the send-off, even though his main reason for doing so was to show off his brand new Kodak Brownie eight millimeter movie camera.

The assembled throng stood in ranks as the filming took place. The Dunstall brothers sat on fold-up chairs in the centre of the front row with a line of employees kneeling either side of them while the second row of workers were standing. Those forming the third row had been made to arrange themselves along the top of the loading bay. Amongst them was a five-year old boy. He had been allowed on the trip by a sympathetic Mr. Michael, because his mother Karen, who worked in accounts, was a single parent who had been let down at the last minute by her child minder.

All involved on this sunny morning were smiling and waving as the camera panned along each row. The employees were dressed in their best 'smart casuals' and some of the older men wore blazers. Mr. Edward and Mr. Stanley had swapped their business suits for sports jackets, brogues and cavalry twills, while Mr. Michael felt a little more adventurous in his oatmeal coloured lightweight jacket with matching trousers.

Most importantly, the Dunstall & Sons company sign, with its happy paint tin couple, could be seen in all its glory on the wall above everyone.

Karen Thomas and her young son Noel were first in the queue of employees to board the second of the two coaches. There were fewer passengers on this coach and most of the trippers were glad of that. It meant more leg room. And travellers on the first full coach would have to put up with boozy antics from the high-kicking team of ladies during the return trip, plus loud and painful renditions of every Stanley Holloway song that ever was.

Mr. Michael had put himself in charge of the seating arrangements and had allowed Karen and her son to occupy the front seats opposite the driver so that they would have the best view.

When both coaches were ready for the off, Mr. Michael took his seat behind the driver. This allowed him to give instructions. It also provided him with the chance to watch Karen. He had admired her from afar for so long. And now here was the opportunity to be close to her, but not so close as to appear foolish.

On boarding the coach Karen had smiled warmly at him and thanked him for letting them have the front seats. She had also told him how smart he looked in his summer suit. He wondered if she was flirting just a bit. Or was this his imagination? Either way, it had charmed him. And he continued to watch her as she pointed things out to the child who was busily peering from the window and waving to the people they passed. Mr. Michael thought yet again how pretty Karen was and wondered why the father of her child would ever have wanted to leave them. Yet he was fully aware that for the time being the object of his desire would have to remain out of reach. He reminded himself that there was the age difference to be taken into consideration, plus, even in these enlightened times, his social status within the company, although he had hope for what the future might bring.

Gate Town Gazette – Friday August 11, 1961 –
Obituaries
Miss Karen Thomas
24 year old Karen Anne Thomas, who sadly died in a tragic accident on August 5th last was born and brought up in Gate Town. A pretty young woman, who had unfortunately been burdened with domestic responsibilities for most of her short life, she will be sadly missed by all those who knew her…

As the second coach followed the lead coach along Ferry Lane, there was a lot of jolly banter on board and someone began to sing, far too early, 'Oh, I do like to be beside the seaside,' but was shouted down by cries of 'we're not there yet,' causing even more merriment.

Sitting directly behind Karen and her son were twenty-one year old Tony Merrow and fifty-five year old Frank Johnson.

Gate Town Gazette – Friday August 11, 1961 –
Obituaries
Mr. Anthony Merrow

Former schoolboy amateur boxing champion, Anthony John Merrow, only son of Ralph and Mary Merrow of Church Street, Gate Town, was tragically killed on August 5th. A victim of the Dunstall & Sons motor coach accident, twenty-one year old Tony was engaged to be married, and he and his fiancée had been making plans for an Easter wedding....

Mr. Frank Johnson

A well known leading member of Ash Hill bowls club, Frank Jarvis Johnson, also died on August 5th in the Dunstall & Sons holiday coach crash. Frank was fifty-five years old and is survived by Yvonne, his wife of thirty-two years, and their four children....

8

The exercise compound at Charnham Cross had been extended. Extra high sections of chain-link fencing had been put up to create a sealed-off separate recreation area. But, unlike the large, tarmacked area, this smaller compound had been constructed on grass.

It was dusk as security officers stood guard by the opened gates of the new compound. A delivery lorry was reversing its way carefully into the compound and over the grass. Mrs. O'Day was there. A mist was forming and the temperature had dropped considerably. A couple of the guards were rubbing their hands and shrugging their shoulders at the sudden cold snap. But the change in the weather hadn't bothered Mrs. O'Day. She was directing the lorry driver with a brisk waving of her hands.

The lorry eventually came to a halt and the driver and his mate opened the rear of the vehicle. The interior was packed with large boxes and variously sized flat-pack units. The two men began to unload the bulky items.

Pierce walked past on his way to the car park and wondered what the fuck was going on.

Jace had at last taken the brown envelope from the drawer and was about to open it when her entry phone buzzed.

'Who is it?' she asked.

It was Rosa. Jace went down the stairs and found the kid outside in the darkness, tarted up for work yet looking like a waif. And she had a cold.

Rosa jigged up and down on her high heels to keep her feet warm. Her nose was running. 'You working or what?' she asked as she wiped her nose with a big spotted hanky.

Jace looked out at a very cold and misty Ferry Lane. She shivered. 'No. I'm not freezing me tits off on a night like this.'

'Ah, come on, Jace. I don't want to be on me own.'

'I'll think about it,' said Jace, who had no intention of going out. 'See you later.' She closed the door.

Rosa wiped her nose once more. She coughed a wet cough. She tottered off on her high heels into the mist.

Shad was on the prowl on this misty night. He wanted to go to the Cat in the Cradle pub again because that was where some of the teenage girls could be found, but he decided to give it a rest just for a while. He didn't want to draw too much attention to himself just yet after he had lapsed somewhat by doing his 'magical performance' there that evening. This was due to the fact he'd had a few glasses of rum and a sudden desire for the young woman that he'd lifted up in the chair. Oh, he would love to have raised her on high in so many different ways. So he had found a small pub off the beaten track, but the only customers were a couple of old hags and a few sad looking men. The barmaid looked promising, but she was nowhere near young enough or artless enough for him. So he left the rum alone and had a couple of pints of the piss that these Neanderthals drank and decided that tonight he definitely needed someone young again. And he liked them back here in time. They tasted somehow sweeter to him mainly because they were more basic and natural, unlike those in his own time period. Why else would he have jumped ship and stayed in this hellhole? he reminded himself.

Bonner was sitting at his living room table. He had a tumbler of scotch and he jotted down some notes as he listened to a play-back on the voice recorder.

'… did he ever tell you why he came here in the first place?' Pierce's voice asked.

'No,' Annette's voice replied. 'But I've a feeling he'd been living in a part of the world that wasn't very nice. Like a desert or something.'

'Why do you think that?'

'Well, he liked to go to Providence Park almost every day. Not that it's much of a park. And… and garden centres. He'd buy me plants and things. Look what he's made of my back yard.'

'It's a cold night,' called Lesley from the hallway. Bonner paused the tape as Lesley entered the room. She was carrying a basket of clean linen. 'I'm going to switch my bed on while I'm going up. Do you want me to switch yours on?'

'But it's only a quarter past nine,' Bonner protested.

'Early to bed, early to rise,' said Lesley. She put the basket down on the table top and proceeded to shake out and fold the items of linen. She saw the voice recorder. 'What is that?'

PJ Hammond

'Just a recording, love.'

'Part of your work?'

'Yes.'

'You don't usually bring your work home.'

'Things are different now. A different kind of job.'

'Oh, yes. So you said.'

Bonner looked questioningly at her. Surely she knows that, he thought to himself. Surely she hasn't forgotten. Surely she's seen me using this recorder before. He watched her as she continued to fuss about with the linen and wondered, is she really OK? And should they talk to someone? He then found himself asking even more unanswerable questions such as, she's only forty-fucking-two, does she really want to get old this quickly? If so, what happens next? Will she make a sudden mad dash towards dementia? And could he handle that and all that goes with it?

Lesley shook her shoulders and made a shivery noise. 'Such a change in the weather.' she said. She then hummed happily to herself as she finished folding the linen. Bonner watched her and remembered some of their good days together. It made him feel sad. He continued to watch her as she carried the basket out into the hallway and up the stairs.

He returned to his notes and released the pause button.

'And he really admired the trees in the park,' Annette was saying. 'I mean, they're just trees, but he loved them, and the soil, and anything growing. It's funny. Sometimes he seemed like a child let loose.'

'Did he like to visit any other places?'

There was a short pause. Then Annette replied. 'Sometimes he liked to go to the Connaught.'

Bonner's own voice cut in on the tape, 'The cemetery?'

'Yes. God knows why. There's not much to see there, except graves. It's got a few trees, I suppose. And flowers…'

Bonner stopped the tape. He looked up from his notes. He reached for his glass of scotch as he sat there in thought.

'Don't tell me he came back here just to study the fucking landscape,' he said aloud to himself.

It was colder in the side ward at Charnham Cross this evening. Cara was fast asleep in her bed. Eve, with a blanket pulled around her shoulders, was preparing herself for bed before the light was switched to dimmer.

Like David Doughty, Eve had had plenty of

things to reflect on during her enforced stay at Charnham Cross. But since the bout of questioning there was even more for her to be concerned about. Who the hell *was* the man whose photograph she had been shown, she wondered, and who was the dead man? She was still half convinced that it was a trick on her tormentors' part. Surely it had to be a trick, she tried to tell herself, because that was how these people worked. It was what they were trained to do, to just lay traps and watch and wait until a mistake was made, unlike her, who had also been trained not to make mistakes and had failed.

But she reminded herself that not all of it was her fault, because it was all to do with circumstances. As she moved to her bed and sat down upon it she also tried to reassure herself that they couldn't possibly keep her and her child confined here or anywhere else for any great length of time, and she believed and hoped that Mrs. O'Day, was simply trying to scare her. Yet somehow, deep down inside, something nagged away, causing her to doubt this.

The light switched to dimmer. And Eve hated this. She would even have preferred complete darkness to this greyish gloom that went on throughout the night.

It had not been a good night for Rosa. There were

no other girls out and about at the usual pick-up spots in Chain Lane, which was not surprising as the cold mist had graduated to a full-blown fog and it was almost freezing. Her cold was getting worse and she knew she wasn't looking her best because of that. She felt like shit.

A couple of slowly moving cars had slowed to almost a standstill as the drivers took a peek at her. Then both had changed their minds and driven on. Rosa blamed the weather conditions for their lack of interest. Anyway, she was pissed off, and she was all set to go home when she saw someone approaching through the fog.

Up ahead, Shad heard a coughing noise and saw a small figure in the feeble light of a streetlamp. Surely not a schoolgirl, he thought. Not on her own. Not on a night like this. Then, as he grew closer to Rosa, his spirits lifted. It was just a child. A very ordinary looking child with a runny nose and a bad cough, but with a short skirt and a reasonable figure. And she was smiling at him. She was selling herself. He was in luck.

'Hi,' said Rosa. She dabbed at her nose with her sleeve. 'Wanna spend some time with a nice girl?'

'Possibly,' said Shad.

Rosa managed to smile, sniff and cough all at the same time. She indicated. 'I live along there.'

Shad could see nothing through the fog. 'Show me,' he said.

Rosa proceeded to walk in the said direction. Shad walked with her. They eventually crossed to the far pavement. 'So where are your parents?' he asked cautiously.

'Oh, they split up years ago. Went their own ways. I never see 'em.'

'So who do you live with?'

'Me nan.'

Shad stopped abruptly.

'Don't worry,' said Rosa. 'She'll be in bed. And she knows what I do. She won't bother us. She knows I'll buy her something nice tomorrow.' She gave another cough. A more prolonged one this time. 'Sorry about this poxy cold. It's doing the rounds. So where you from? You don't sound like you're from round here.'

'I'm not. I'm from a long way away.'

As they walked on along Chain Lane, various thoughts were running through Shad's mind. He made up his mind that if he was to enjoy himself properly he would have to do something about the little tart's cold. Killing the girl by the cemetery had been a pleasure, yet he was unable to enjoy it to the full because of the risk of being seen. But this was different. This creature was perfect. It was asking for it. It's a shame it wasn't pretty. And the cold made its face look even worse, so something definitely had to be done about that.

Rosa gave another cough then took the hanky from her pocket and blew her nose.

'Here we are,' she croaked as they turned into a narrow street of cramped looking terraced houses.

Shad dwelled once more on his luck and the fact that things were all so easy for him here in the past. So obtainable. And back there, where he'd travelled from, he had been deprived of the kind of love he needed. And whatever the analysts and the law makers thought, to him it definitely was love. A short, brutal, frantic few moments of pleasure and death combined. That was his kind of love. Because he did somehow love them dearly, however fleetingly, during their last few moments.

Rosa stopped at the door of one of the small houses. There were no lights on inside. She took keys from her pocket and opened the door quietly. She then stifled a cough as she beckoned Shad inside. He followed her into the tiny hallway.

'I'm in here,' she said quietly. She glanced up at the dark stairs and then opened the door to a small front room. She ushered Shad in and switched on the light before closing the door carefully.

Shad looked around him. There were two

small armchairs, a sideboard and an opened up but untidy sofa bed. This would have been called the best room in the house, he supposed. If so, he wondered just how squalid the rest of this hovel could be. He guessed that an historian travelling back from his time period would enthuse over it. But not him.

Rosa switched on a small bedside lamp, turned off the main light, then removed her coat. 'Make yourself comfortable,' she said as she straightened the bedclothes. She coughed once more, then blew and wiped her nose yet again. She turned to see that Shad was still standing there. 'You not gonna get undressed then?' she asked, unbuttoning her blouse.

Shad smiled at her. 'I'd like to do something for you first.'

'Like what?'

'I'd like to get rid of that cold of yours.'

'How?'

'I'll show you.' He reached into the inside pocket of his coat and took out a tiny sachet. It reminded Rosa of the kind of sauce sachet that you get in a café, except that it was smaller and glittery.

'So what are you, a doctor or something?' she asked as she kicked off her shoes and pulled down her skirt. 'Only I don't need no doctor.'

'No, I'm not a doctor.'

Rosa stopped what she was doing. Remembering all the warnings given by Jace and the other girls about iffy clients, she looked carefully at Shad.

Shad smiled again as he gave the sachet a good shake. 'I'm just a comforter in times of need.'

'I'm not drinking nothing.'

'Oh, you don't have to drink this. It's a salve.'

'A what?'

'It cures most things. Your cold will be gone in no time. Where I come from no-one has a cold.'

'Lucky them,' said Rosa.

She still looked unsure. Shad saw this. He knew he didn't want to scare her. He didn't want mayhem. Not yet. He pretended to be about to leave. 'Oh, well. Maybe another time.'

'No,' said Rosa quickly. 'It's all right.' She decided to take the chance. She'd wasted an evening in that cold, shitty lane and she needed the money. 'So what do I do?'

'First, just listen to me.'

Rosa nodded.

'This is a new kind of medication. So it may seem strange to you at first.'

Rosa nodded once more.

'But just relax. Let it happen.' He rubbed the

sachet between his fingers to open it. 'Sit on the bed.'

Rosa sat on the bed.

'Lean back'.

Rosa leant back.

'Head on the pillow.'

Rosa rested her head on the pillow.

'Close your eyes.'

'I'm not closing my eyes.'

'Just for a second or two. It only takes that long.'

Rosa considered this for a moment. She then closed her eyes. Shad held the sachet over her face. Two or three shiny drops of clear liquid, that had the consistency of quicksilver, fell on to Rosa's forehead and spread swiftly over her face like a transparent, shimmering mask.

But relaxing was out of the question for Rosa. Startled by the sudden sensation she screamed and the scream bubbled through the mask on her face. She continued to scream and the scream became louder and more panicky. As far as Shad was concerned, it was enough to wake the whole street. From upstairs, there was a clattering noise and a woman's voice called out. Shad shoved the empty sachet back in his pocket. He moved quickly to the door and into the hallway as the screaming continued.

The landing light had come on and a frightened old lady was descending the stairs. Shad decided there and then to kill the pair of them. But first he eased open the front door and peered out to see if the noise had roused the neighbours. It had. As the loud screaming continued, lights from open doors were shining through the fog, a dog was barking furiously and the vague shapes of people could be seen. Shad flung open the door and made a run for it.

As he ran, Shad decided that this was the last time he'd go out of his way to help these creatures, even if it was to his own advantage. As he turned into Chain Lane and hid momentarily from a passing vehicle, he vowed he would simply kill them in future. Just have his fun and kill them. And at least he now knew where to find the young tarts should he need one.

In the front room of the small house, Rosa stopped screaming. The clear mask was evaporating from her face. The old woman had entered the room. She was still frightened and concerned for her grandchild. But Rosa hadn't noticed. She sat on the bed looking surprised as she touched at her face. Her head and throat had cleared.

'This is crazy,' she said. She then realised that her voice was also back to normal. 'My cold. It's gone.'

9

Although it was less cold, the fog had hung around Gate Town for a further two days, making the early morning rush hour less of a rush but even more of a snarl-up than usual. So Bonner was not in a good mood as he was forced to drive at more or less walking speed across town.

Earlier that morning he had pressed Jace's door buzzer but had received no reply. He couldn't understand this. Jace never slept late. And she didn't believe in having overnight clients. Some time ago she had taken his advice and given him spare keys to the flat. But she had insisted that he only used them in an emergency because she had a living to make. So Bonner decided against entering the flat at this moment in time, but planned to come back later.

At nine-forty-five he was still driving slowly

through the town centre in nose-to-tail traffic. He saw one of Jace's colleagues emerging from the fog. She was heading for the launderette with a bag of washing. He wound his window down and called, 'Fran? You seen Jace?'

'No,' said Fran. 'She wasn't out all weekend.'

Inside the new compound at Charnham Cross several members of the security squad had been put to work removing tarpaulin covers from the large assortment of flat-packs and unpacking and assembling the contents, which proved to be assorted lengths of timber, sections of plastic, lengths of rope, and clear plastic bags full of nuts, bolts, washers and various other fiddly items. There was also a substantial looking instruction manual on how to put whatever it was together. The security officers were not exactly happy to be given this task, especially in fog, but no-one dared argue. As always, Mrs. O'Day's word was law. So it was either get on with it or be given a fast track transfer to somewhere less desirable. And with Christmas looming it wasn't a good time to be on the move.

Bonner eventually arrived at his destination, the Connaught. He parked his car, took a walk through the fog-bound cemetery and found that he agreed with Annette. Why would David Doughty want to visit this Godforsaken place? Why would anyone? He felt that most cemeteries had a kind of sad, sedate charm. But the Connaught had neither of these, especially on a morning such as this, which was made worse by the impatient engine sounds from slowed-down traffic on the nearby ring road. It was dear old Gate Town enjoying yet another noisy, crappy morning, and Bonner made up his mind that when his days as a longstanding local resident came to an end, he wasn't going to end up here at the Connaught.

Accompanied by his guard, David Doughty pushed his wheelbarrow of gardening tools around the side of the main compound. He then stopped as, through the fog, he saw figures moving in the smaller compound and glimpsed some kind of strange structure being assembled.

Princess Mary Road was on the edge of Gate Town and looked as out-of-date as its name suggested. Due to the ongoing development projects, the road and its neighbouring thoroughfares had been earmarked for demolition for some time. As a result of this, most of the homeowners had accepted the council's measly offer for the sale of their properties and their little red brick houses were now boarded-up, with the security boards having been duly decorated with graffiti. But a few of the residents were misguidedly sticking out for a better offer that they were never going to get.

Two such homeowners were Raymond and Sylvia Pearson of number fifty-three Princess Mary Road. They were in their early sixties and had been running their home as a B&B for the past twenty-five years. Of course, the road wasn't too appealing these days. In fact, it looked semi-derelict. But Raymond and Sylvia did their best to keep number fifty-three looking alive and well from the outside by keeping the net half curtains on the downstairs front windows nice and clean, and always making sure the 'B&B' and 'Vacancies' signs were in place. But they were wasting their time. The milkmen and newspaper shops no longer delivered to Princess Mary Road because it wasn't worth their while. So either Raymond or Sylvia had to drive off to collect necessary items in their little Renault Clio, which they kept parked round the back in the rear alleyway just for safety's sake.

Sylvia could best be described as neat but dowdy. Yet she would have been a pretty woman once upon a time. And sometimes, when she smiled, glimpses of that prettiness could still be seen. But Sylvia rarely smiled these days.

Raymond was sallow faced and his ginger hair was now mostly grey and thinning. He seemed almost always to wear clothes that matched his complexion, his favourite colours being beige, biscuit or sand. Some time ago, when they still had friends, one of them had made a joke about Raymond lying down in the desert and never being seen again. He and Sylvia never quite saw the joke. And yet the desert was all set to come to them quite soon, in the shape of dumper trucks and pneumatic drills and wrecking balls.

The B&B once had a steady trickle of guests, mostly salesmen, until the area was surveyed. Then people stopped coming. But Raymond and Sylvia had been lucky of late. About a couple of months ago an out-of-town visitor had come to stay, and he was still with them. He had signed in as Mr. J. Silks and had described himself as an entertainer who specialized in illusionism.

From what Raymond and Sylvia could make out, their guest was a well travelled man, although he didn't appear to have much in the way of luggage. But he had explained that he was on a recce and planned to eventually live full time in Gate Town. He was a polite, tidy person who sometimes came in late, but never made a nuisance of himself. And, because they were badly in need of his custom, Raymond and Sylvia allowed him to use his room during certain hours of the day if he wished, providing this didn't interfere with their domestic duties.

Raymond had at first wondered if there was any call for illusionists in a place like Gate Town. But Sylvia was impressed with the man, so he decided not to raise the subject with her.

Their gentleman guest had come down to breakfast that morning and Sylvia had served him with coffee, and eggs and tomatoes on toast as usual. She peered over the top of the half net curtains. 'Not as bad out there now,' she said. 'Fog seems to be lifting.'

'Good,' said Shad. He smiled warmly at her.

Nurse Claire accompanied Eve and Cara as they walked from the hospital shower room at Charnham Cross. Mother and child's hair was wet. Eve carried towels over her shoulder. They passed through the empty main ward.

'Got something to show you, Cara,' said Claire. 'Come and see.' She led the child to one of the windows that still had bars in place from the old days. She lifted her up so that she could see from the window. 'Look'.

Cara looked. The fog was indeed lifting a little and whatever was being constructed in the smaller compound had now been finished and could at last be seen through the misty air. Looking completely out of place in this next best thing to an internment camp was a children's 'Happy Times' activity centre. In the centre was a tall wooden tower with a platform and a pitched roof. Jutting out from the tower was a beam, supported at its opposite end by an A-frame. Various pieces of playground apparatus hung from the beam, including a rope ladder, a swing and a suspended rubber tyre. Fixed to the back of the tower was a slide, and to the front was a wooden climbing frame. The tower also had an array of smaller things attached to it. There were colourful handles, rings, knobs, bells, wheels and plastic animals. To one side of the tower was a sandpit, and on the opposite side stood a small roundabout.

Cara smiled and stared in wonder at this bizarre sight. Eve moved to the window. She also looked out. But what she saw did not please her. In fact, it had the opposite effect. To her, it was a threat. She foresaw the possibility of more to come in the shape of new buildings and improved accommodation, because she had not forgotten Mrs. O'Day's threat that she and her daughter could be in this terrible place forever.

Claire set Cara back down on her feet. The child looked pleased. She turned to Eve. 'Mama, I like it here,' she said. Then, to the nurse. 'When can I play?'

Before Claire could answer, Eve confronted her. 'Mrs. O'Day. Where is she?'

'I'm not sure.'

'Well, I want to see her. Now.'

With the fog now sparse, Bonner was able to get a better look at the cemetery. It was a vast area, filled with row upon row of Gate Town's dead. There were long forgotten, well weathered graves and more recent ones. There were plain ones, ugly ones and over elaborate ones. Due to subsidence over the years, some of the very old gravestones had reared up out of the ground, or were partly sunk into the earth, with their assorted columns and crosses tilted at odd angles. To Bonner, it looked like the aftermath of some old tank battle.

Apart from the fact that the dead downtimer had been found close by, Bonner could find nothing here that seemed to show a link between David Doughty and the cemetery. Of course, he could spend several days searching every inch of the place, but what was the point?

On the way back to his car he walked to the nearby lane where the schoolgirl had been murdered. So far, DNA tests had proved inconclusive, yet the Major Crime Unit were still at work on the case. Bonner was not surprised at the slowness of the investigation. He had always felt that there were no star players or gifted mavericks within the unit, and if they were relying on the support of the local division, which included Prior Street nick, then things would stay that way.

He stopped and looked at the exact spot where the girl was killed. Some ripped and dirtied strips of police marker tape remained in place. In lieu of flowers, to Bonner they seemed to represent a sad and grubby epitaph to the poor kid. He was also aware that the site was no more than thirty or forty yards from where the downtimer had met his end, and he thought that at least the unfortunate girl was a child of today and not some crazy-arsed escapee from the future. It reminded him of what Mrs. O'Day had asked and would continue to ask. Why the fuck do they come to Gate Town?

His mobile rang. It was Mrs. O'Day. 'You'd better get back here, Sol,' she said. 'The lady wants to talk.'

Nurse Claire stood watching as Cara clambered happily up the climbing frame of the activity centre tower. She toyed with some of the gaudily coloured accessories. She then gave a whoop of pleasure as she slid down the bright orange slide, before hopping and skipping her way to the rope ladder.

In the early days, Mrs. O'Day had chosen the least run-down office room at Charnham Cross. She was no mug. She had then had it decorated and fitted out to suit her needs. And she had asked for, and been provided with, the largest and most state-of-the-art desk on offer. The office also had its surveillance camera and interview recorder.

Mrs. O'Day was sitting at her desk as Bonner and Pierce led Eve into the room. Once more, Eve seemed faintly amused by the procedure as Bonner switched on the recorder.

'Is something funny?' asked Mrs. O'Day as she invited Eve to sit down. 'Only we can't help being a wee bit behind the times. It's a cross we have to bear. So, apart from manufactured eyesight, what else can we look forward to in the future? In your future?'

Eve said nothing.

'Come on, surprise us. It can't do any harm,

can it?' she indicated the recorder. 'How do your people save information?'

Eve thought about this before holding up one hand. She indicated the palm. 'Memory lifelines. For those who don't like serious operations.' She touched her head. 'Otherwise it's brain grafts for academics, lawyers and similar professions.'

'And do you have one of these grafts?'

Eve said nothing.

'We can check. Give you another examination.'

'Then you'll be wasting your time. Mine won't operate this far back in time. Therefore it's been deactivated. Apart from which, your kind of technology would fail to locate it.'

Mrs. O'Day reached for her cigarettes and lighter. She lit up. 'You've asked to see me.'

'Yes. There was something I forgot to tell you when you last questioned me. I was hoping someone from Timelight would follow me back. Support me.'

'Support you in what way?'

'Bring me supplies. Give me information. Not leave me and my child stranded.'

'And what sort of someone would that be? Another one of your jolly field trippers?'

Eve ignored the remark.

'We showed you a photograph.'

'I didn't recognise him. Have there been others?'

'Not as far as we know.'

Eve sat there in silence for a moment. She looked at the watchful faces of Bonner, Pierce and Mrs. O'Day. They were giving away nothing.

'I don't want my daughter to spend the rest of her life in a prison. Why can't we be integrated into your society? We won't cause trouble.'

'I've already explained it to you,' Mrs. O'Day replied. 'You've caused trouble by coming here in the first place. And we don't do human rights. Not here. We don't need to.'

Before Eve could respond, Mrs. O'Day continued. 'So, apart from informing us how wonderfully advanced you people are, what else can you tell us? Are you sure you can't remember how you arrived here? Maybe you've had some thoughts since we last spoke. Maybe some little recollections have come trickling back through that memory lifeline of yours, or whatever other built-in bodily delights you might have.'

'I've told you over and over again,' said Eve. 'Nothing changes. I was asleep. We have to be asleep. It doesn't work otherwise.' She looked at Bonner. 'The one who died. What did you do with him?'

'He's still here.'

Eve was unsettled by this. She feared it was a trick. 'You mean he's been buried?'

Bonner did not answer.

'Were you hoping he may have been the one sent back to find you?' asked Mrs. O'Day.

'Yes,' said Eve.

'Well, let's hope he was. Otherwise it means your history-loving chums have really screwed up on you.' Mrs. O'Day paused for a moment before asking, 'Would you like to see him?'

Eve looked puzzled. 'See him? How?'

Mrs. O'Day stubbed out her cigarette butt. She looked at Bonner and Pierce. 'Show her,' she said. 'I've got things to do.' Pierce got up from his chair. Bonner switched off the recorder.

Bonner, Pierce and Eve walked across the old parade ground to the confinement block. At the far side of the ground David Doughty was hard at work. He was kneeling down and had made a start on clearing the weeds that had managed to fight their way up through the surfaces of the cracked asphalt and concrete. It was going to be a long, hard job.

Doughty, in his category A kit, looked up as he noticed Eve, similarly dressed, being walked across the parade ground. She saw him as she passed. The man from the photograph. A complete stranger. It worried Eve.

The three walked on until they reached the blockhouse. Pierce took his set of keys from his pocket and unlocked a door on the ground floor. They entered. Pierce then led the way up a flight of stairs to a large open area on the first floor. Since the appearance of the first downtimer, the area had been hurriedly cleaned up and turned into a temporary mortuary. Plumbing had been hastily provided and post mortem equipment brought in.

Eve looked uneasily around her. 'What is this place?' she asked.

'You should find it interesting, Mrs. Palmer,' said Pierce, with a wry smile. 'It has a history.'

Eve remained uneasy as they crossed the expanse of newly laminated floor, passing a post mortem table, sinks, scales and a couple of trolleys.

'Used to be a gymnasium for military prisoners in peace time,' Pierce continued. 'In war time it was a place of execution.'

Eve grimaced.

The trio reached a set of double doors at the very end of the mortuary area and Pierce stopped. He pointed at a section of the floor beneath them. 'The old scaffold trapdoors are under here.'

Eve involuntarily stepped back, and Pierce gave another humourless smile. 'Don't worry. They were sealed up long ago.' He used another key to unlock the doors of the adjoining room. 'And this is where those due for execution were kept. Their last place of shelter on this earth.'

He opened the doors to a bright, white, windowless room. The only object in the room was also white. It was a large, forbidding looking cold-room module. Pierce entered the room but Eve had hesitated in the doorway.

Bonner took Eve by the arm and spoke quietly. 'You'll be OK. Just take it easy with this.' Eve nodded and allowed Bonner to lead her into the room.

'We've made all the examinations we need to make,' said Pierce as he began to unlatched the doors of the module. 'But we still know little about him.' A blast of cold air filled the room as Pierce opened wide the module doors. 'Would you please take a look, Mrs. Palmer?'

Eve hesitated once more.

'A close look.'

Bonner took Eve's arm once more and walked her to the module. She shivered at the cold air. She then stopped immediately and gave a choked cry of horror.

It was a walk-in cold-room. The left and right hand racks were empty. But in the walkway a power stacking trolley had been adjusted so that a body tray upon it was set at an almost upright angle and facing the doors. The naked body of the D.O.A. downtimer was strapped to the tray.

Eve stared at the open-eyed, dead face of the man who called himself Joseph Valentine. He was a stranger to her. But she recognised his kind. It was the lean, muscular body of someone who had once kept himself physically fit, plus there were the tell-tale, check-patterned signs of scar tissue.

'Do you recognise him?' asked Pierce.

Eve shook her head. She began to shudder.

'What about those scar tissues? Can you tell us what they are? Because pretty soon we'll need to take skin samples before we put him into deep freeze.'

Still in shock, Eve failed to answer. She turned away. She felt faint. She stumbled. Bonner reached out and steadied her.

Mrs. O'Day did indeed have things to do. It was still cold, but a wintry sun was at last shining as she walked from the administration building and made her way towards the smaller compound. Cara was busy playing in the sand pit. She was using a child's yellow plastic bucket and red plastic spade.

Nurse Claire unlocked the compound gate and Mrs. O'Day entered. She watched Cara at play for a moment before wandering towards the sand pit.

'Hello, Cara,' she said. Cara looked up. Mrs. O'Day indicated the activity centre. 'Like all this, do you?'

'Yes,' said Cara as she continued to fill her bucket with sand.

'Thought you would,' said Mrs. O'Day. 'That's why we got it for you. So what do you say?'

'Thank you,' said Cara.

'Did you have one of these at home?'

Cara shook her head. 'We didn't have a garden.'

'No. Your other home. The one you lived in before you came here.'

Cara shook her head once more. She threw down the plastic spade and ran to the climbing frame.

'Do you remember coming here from that other home?'

'Yes,' said Cara as she climbed up into the tower.

'So what do you remember?'

'Mama said I wasn't to say.'

'Oh, your mama won't mind you talking to me.'

Cara said nothing. She slid down the slide. Mrs. O'Day strolled over to meet her at the end of the slide.

'Surely you must remember some little things?'

Cara shook her head yet again. She climbed on to the swing. Mrs. O'Day moved to the swing. She began to push the swing gently. 'Did you come here by bus?'

Cara giggled as she swung to and fro. 'No.'

'Or by train?'

Cara giggled even more. 'Trains can't come all this way, silly.'

'No, of course they can't,' agreed Mrs. O'Day. She released the swing. Cara climbed from it. She moved back to the sandpit.

'Anyway, your mama has already told me. She said you were both asleep when you first came here. Is that right?'

Cara nodded. She tipped out the sand from the bucket in a steady trickle.

'So you didn't see anything?'

Cara began to fill up the bucket once more. 'Only a picture.'

'What sort of picture?'

'Just a picture.' She sprinkled more sand from the bucket. 'And there was a light.'

'A light?'

'It hurt my eyes. Then I was asleep.'

She threw away the bucket and ran to the roundabout. She struggled to push it. Mrs. O'Day moved to help. She lifted the child and sat her on the roundabout seat.

'Did you see anything else?'

'Just a ghost,' said Cara. 'Just a funny little ghost.'

Gate Town Gazette – Friday August 11, 1961 –
Obituaries
Noel Thomas
Noel Timothy Thomas, five year old son of Karen
Thomas, who was killed in a coach crash on August 5th,
sadly died of his injuries on August 8th....

10

The old staff canteen at Charnham Cross had been brought back to life when Mrs. O'Day first took over. New ovens, fridges and freezers had been installed and a couple of chefs from the Royal Logistic Corps had been given postings at the camp.

There was a Christmas tree and some decorations were being hung up above the serving counter. Bonner looked at them as he queued for coffee and a bun. He was not a fan of Christmas.

Pierce was already sitting at a table as Bonner joined him. He set down his mug of coffee and bun. Mrs. O'Day entered the canteen she walked directly to the table.

'So she didn't recognise the body?'

'No', said Pierce.

'Was she lying? She seems to be good at that.'

Pierce shook his head. 'I don't think she was lying. Not this time.'

'I agree', said Bonner, tucking into his bun. 'Do you want a coffee?'

'No,' said Mrs. O'Day. She pulled out a chair and sat down at the table. She sat there in thought for a moment or two. 'A picture, a light, and a small ghost.'

Pierce was puzzled. 'What?'

'That's what the little girl said she saw, the moment she was sent back from her own time period.'

Bonner stopped eating his bun. 'She told you that?'

'Yes.'

'Why? How?'

'Because I've been taking it down to her level, that's how. Why d'you think I built a bloody playground out there?'

'The kid's only four years old,' said Bonner.

'That doesn't matter. She said it.'

'But the other two have insisted they were asleep,' said Pierce. 'Maybe the child was dreaming.'

Mrs. O'Day said nothing. She remained in thought for a moment. She reached out for Bonner's coffee mug.

'That's got sugar in,' said Bonner.

'That's all right.' Mrs. O'Day drank some of the coffee then set the mug down beside her. 'Give me your notebook.'

Bonner took a notebook and pen from his pocket. He handed them to Mrs. O'Day. She drew a small square with a squiggle in it on the first page. She then drew a light bulb on the second page and a wavy white sheet with two round eyes on the third. She tore each page from the notebook and placed them down on the table top, like playing cards, saying, 'Picture. Light. Ghost. Now let's think about it.'

Bonner and Pierce looked at the pieces of paper.

'Symbols of some kind?' said Pierce.

'Could be,' said Mrs. O'Day. 'Or apparatus. Part of the apparatus they used.'

Pierce thought about this. 'If it got them here, could it get them back?'

Mrs. O'Day wasn't sure. 'If it could, don't you think our Mrs. Palmer would have tried it? And if there was such a piece of apparatus, where would they have hidden the bloody thing?'

Bonner turned the pieces of paper this way and that. He then realigned them before putting them back as they were. 'A photograph?' he wondered.

'A what?'

'Well, maybe whoever sent them back took

a photo of the moment it happened. Just for the record.'

Mrs. O'Day looked unimpressed as Bonner continued, 'And if it all happened in a fraction of a second while the kid was half asleep it could have looked like these to her.' He tapped at the three notebook pages.

'That doesn't make sense,' said Pierce.

'Of course it doesn't make sense,' said Mrs. O'Day. 'You heard what the lady said, with her memory lifelines and her brain grafts. You've seen the post mortem report on the dead downtimer. We all know that they've travelled back. We don't know how, but they've done it. We're talking about over a hundred years in the future, for Christ's sake. Why would they use something as ancient as a camera?'

'That had occurred to me,' said Bonner, with an edge to his voice.

'Good. I'm glad to hear it.'

'Yeah, well maybe they just *thought* their fucking way back here,' said Bonner as he got up from the table, grabbed his pen and notebook and walked to the door.

Mrs. O'Day said nothing. She finished the rest of his coffee.

Bonner left the administration building and made his way to the car park. He had nothing but respect for Mrs. O'Day, but now and again she just wore him down, and when that happened he needed to put a bit of breathing space between them for a short while. And Mrs. O'Day knew this. She understood it. It had happened before and it would happen again, and more often than not it improved their working relationship. Of course, being worried about Jace didn't help. Bonner knew that was why he had snapped. That and Mrs. O'Day's usual put-down bitchiness. Right now he didn't need that.

'OK, I got it wrong by suggesting a photograph,' he muttered as he opened his car door. 'So fucking what?'

It was lunchtime at the Gantry when Bonner looked in. He found it surprisingly busy for mid-day on a Monday, and guessed it was probably some medico-cum-legal do because there were a lot of suits gathered around, with a smattering of tweed here and there, and he recognised a few people from his divisional CID days.

The atmosphere was hearty and chatty and a bit too noisy, and Bonner had to raise his voice to order a half of bitter and ask about Jace. But Clumpy Ron said he hadn't seen her since Thursday.

Bonner was now seriously concerned. Hoping she hadn't gone back on her word and was trying to hurt herself again, he decided to go straight back to her flat and let himself in. He downed half of his beer during an even louder burst of shouty laughter from the assembled suits and tweeds, then found Allie, wearing a smart, two-piece skirt suit, standing next to him. She was holding a glass of orange juice and she had a big smile on her face.

'I shouldn't be here.' She almost had to shout as a thunderous round of applause erupted from the suits. 'But I slipped away.'

'Me, too,' said Bonner, trying to make himself heard. 'Don't worry. I won't tell.' Allie gave another smile. Bonner had to half yell the question, 'You with that lot?'

Allie nodded, still smiling. She then led Bonner to the far end of the bar where it was a little quieter. 'We're forensic, most of us,' she said. 'A lot of us studied together. And there's a couple from SOCO.' She pointed at a man in the throng. 'And you must know Don Martin, deputy coroner.'

'Yeah, I know him. So what are you celebrating?'

Allie pointed in the direction of another man who was making what appeared to be a brief but lively speech. 'Simon. Pathologist at Saint Mary's. It's his retirement do. The only time I get to see all my old crowd is when there's a retirement or a funeral.'

The speech had finished and there was another noisy round of applause and some cheers. Allie turned to join in with the hand clapping. It gave Bonner yet another chance to admire her shape. He thought she looked even taller in her going-out shoes, and the high heels gave her bigness even more thrust.

A member of the group made his way to join Allie. He was a mournful looking man. Not so much a smart suit, but more of a sad suit with mismatching tie. His name was Kenneth and he couldn't keep his eyes off Allie. Bonner recognised him as a member of a local forensic science team that worked with the divisional police. It was also obvious to Bonner that while his own appreciation of Allie was mostly lust, Kenneth's seemed to be total adoration.

'Can I get you another drink?' he asked her, without bothering to acknowledge Bonner.

'No, I'm all right, thanks, Ken,' said Allie.

Kenneth gave an obsequious smile. It was as if refusal was a normal part of his life, and if Allie was doing the refusing that was good enough for him. It was better than nothing.

Bonner decided to interrupt this creepy little

exhibition of worship. 'Have your people got any further with that young girl's murder?'

Kenneth turned his head just slightly. He wasn't really interested in talking to Bonner, not when there was Allie to gaze at. 'They're still working on it,' he replied.

'Thought as much,' said Bonner. He gave Allie a grin and a wink as he finished his beer and set down his empty glass. 'Catch up with you.'

'Right, Sir,' said Allie. 'See you later.'

Kenneth watched suspiciously as Bonner made his way to the door. 'Thought he was a sergeant. You called him Sir. '

'He's an Inspector, these days.'

'Oh.' Kenneth was interested. 'One of your oppoes now?'

'Yes.'

'So? This special unit of yours, what exactly is it?'

'Kind of border police,' Allie lied.

'But we're nowhere near the coast.'

'Now they tell me.' Allie looked at her watch. 'Sorry, Ken. Gotta go.'

As Bonner drove back along Ferry Lane to Jace's flat he realised that something was different. It was too quiet. The demolition sounds that had blighted the lane for the past few days could no longer be heard. The sounds were there all right when he first arrived early this morning. But now the pneumatic drills were silent. And before he could get to Jace's place he was met by a barrier of 'road closed' and 'diversion' signs. He stopped his car, climbed from it and made his way past the barrier.

The demolition workers who had stopped work were gathered around a makeshift brazier. They smoked fags and drank tea from flasks as they looked up at the remains of the old paint factory. Members of the public, plus some toddlers dressed in scarves and warm coats, had also gathered and were staring up at the structure. A few of the small kids were clambering around on heaped up rubble.

Supposedly keeping the crowd at bay were two police constables from Prior Street nick. Bonner reckoned the younger one had probably not long left cadet college, while his companion, an old hand who he had seen from time to time but never met, was leaning against the cab of a contractor's lorry.

Bonner approached, then stopped and looked up. The top of the building now seemed as if it had been hit by bombs. And it looked dangerously unsafe. But there was no-one to be seen up there. He moved to take a closer look.

143

'Keep back,' ordered the old hand copper.

'What's going on?' asked Bonner.

'A jumper,' said the rookie.

Bonner looked up once more, shielding his eyes from the winter sun that shone above the drifting smoke from the brazier. 'Where?'

'Right up the top. Keeps hiding, then popping out.'

'Wish she'd fucking jump and get it over with,' said the old hand as he lit a cigarette and held it in a cupped hand. 'Then we can all get back to work.'

Bonner looked at the man. He knew his type. He had that know-all look of someone who has never made it past constable and never would. And he probably told people that that was all he ever wanted. The lying bastard.

'So what are you doing about it?'

'What d'you mean, what are we doing about it?' said the old hand in a weary tone of voice, without even looking at Bonner.

'We've called the emergency services, and there's a negotiator on the way,' said the rookie.

'Waste of fucking time,' said his colleague.

There was a burst of excited chatter from the onlookers.

'She's popped out again,' said the rookie.

Bonner looked up once more. He could see a

figure silhouetted against the sun at the very top of the dodgy looking structure. The figure moved towards the edge and some bricks and rubble and dust came falling down. There were 'Oohs!' and 'Ahs!' from the onlookers. The figure then sat down on the edge.

Without the sun at her back, the figure became clearer. Bonner saw the movement of a pale blue PVC coat.

It was Jace.

Bonner was struck with fear. 'Oh, Christ!' he said aloud.

Jace was now swinging her legs to and fro like a kid on a garden wall as she surveyed the people down below. She then saw Bonner. She waved. She called down to him.

'Hello, Sol!'

People turned to look at Bonner. The two coppers stared at him.

'You know that stupid bitch?' asked the old hand.

But Bonner was already running towards the wrecked building. A demolition foreman intercepted him. 'Can't go in there, mate.'

Bonner snatched his warrant card from his pocket and showed it. 'What's the safest way up?'

'None of it's that safe. But don't use the main

staircase whatever you do. Use what's left of the emergency stairs.' The foreman grabbed a white hard hat that was hanging on a parked dumper truck. 'Here.' He threw the hat to Bonner.

Bonner had to make his way tentatively over accumulated debris in order to enter the building. He put on the hat then picked his way carefully over even more rubble as he looked up at the wrecked building. He was trying not to remind himself that he didn't like heights. And he recalled the time when he was a lad and he'd climbed on a ladder to clear his granddad's gutters. He'd almost come a cropper. And the old man was living in a bungalow at the time. Since then he'd obviously had some challenging moments working for the force, but somehow he'd always managed to get the more agile or foolhardy companions to do the daredevil stuff.

He had to pull aside pieces of smashed woodwork to get to the emergency stairs. A lot of the steps had gone and lengths of handrail were missing. And there was more rubble to be clambered over, so it took him a while to climb those stairs. He also realised that it was a December day, yet he was sweating heavily. He stopped on the remains of a landing to get his breath back. He removed the hard hat, wiped the sweat from his face, then put the hat back on. The front wall of the landing had collapsed. Bonner peered cautiously out and realised that he'd climbed up quite a way. He could see upturned faces watching from the ground, and right now that ground seemed a long way down to him. Yet there was still another flight of stairs to climb.

The last flight of stairs, strewn with rubble and shards of broken glass, proved to be a slow and hazardous climb for Bonner because there was no longer a handrail and the supporting wall looked as if it could give way at any moment. So he had to climb most of it on his hands and knees. Crouching to ease himself under a fallen concrete lintel, he lost the hard hat. It fell from his head and he heard it clattering and banging its way down to the lower floors.

By the time Bonner reached the last piece of busted stair he was completely knackered. The top floor of the building no longer had a roof in place and only the back wall and one side wall were left standing. And they didn't look too healthy. Neither did the floor, which had great gaping holes in it.

Bonner squeezed himself through a broken doorway and stopped. Everything around him seemed so perilous that he hung on to the doorframe for dear life. He could see Jace still sitting on the edge of an open area where the front wall had been. She had her back to him.

'What the fuck are you doing, Jace?'

Jace half turned to look at him. She didn't have that mischievous look that she sometimes had when she was having people on just for effect. There was no fun in her face. Not today. It made Bonner decide to play it calmly.

'Please, Jace. Just get up carefully and come here.'

Jace did not reply. She turned back to look at the ground below her. Bonner thought about making his way towards her, but the large holes in the floor made him change his mind.

'I thought you said you'd given up trying to hurt yourself.'

'I have,' said Jace.

'Then what are you doing up here?'

'I had this letter.'

'What letter?'

'They're gonna stop me benefit.'

At first, Bonner couldn't quite believe what he'd heard. Then he realised he did quite believe it, because it was Jace who was saying it. And nothing was new. Not with Jace.

'That letter. It's probably just a warning, that's all.' Bonner wasn't sure about this, but he wasn't going to argue the odds about the illegal claiming of benefits, not right now. 'It's nothing to worry about.'

'You see, sometimes I worry about a lot of things, Sol.'

'What kind of things?'

'I dunno.'

'Tell me.'

'I worry about where I live.' Jace eased her legs back from the edge of the building and began to get to her feet. 'And some of the people I have to deal with'

'Then don't deal with them any more,' said Bonner. 'Get a kosher job. Move to another part of Gate Town.'

Jace looked at the ground below once more then swayed unsteadily. From below there were concerned cries from some of the onlookers.

'Jace!' shouted Bonner. Then quieter. Calmly. Almost pleading. 'Please, Jace.'

Still expressionless, Jace turned slowly to look at him. At a distance the siren sounds of emergency vehicles could be heard approaching.

Bonner held out a hand. 'Come away from there. Please.'

Jace thought about this for a moment. She then moved away from the edge and began to gingerly tip-toe her way around the holes in the floor. Some of the sections gave way and fell below with a crash and a cloud of dust.

'Jesus!' cried Bonner.

He wanted to move to help her but found he was incapable of letting go of the door frame. Jace was now moving slowly but surely, with her arms held out horizontally like a tightrope walker. She reached Bonner and he grabbed her with his free hand. She looked at his torn and bedraggled clothes.

'It's all right,' said Bonner. 'I never did like this suit.'

'Sorry,' Jace said. She leant forward to give him a peck on the cheek, then pulled back. 'You're all fucking sweaty.'

'Of course I'm fucking sweaty. I've been worried to death about you. And I don't do heights. Never have. And I've still got to get back down.'

'Don't worry about it.' Jace put an arm around him. 'Just hold on to me.'

Bonner continued to cling to the door frame.

'Let go, will you?'

Bonner let go of the door frame. He felt like a cripple being helped across a road as he allowed Jace to take his arm and lead him down the shattered staircase. The sounds of the emergency vehicles could be heard arriving outside. There was a babble of voices and the rattle and clang of equipment.

'You're right,' said Jace, in thought. 'I'll do it. I'll leave Ferry Lane. I don't want to be nearly suffocated or scarred for life by some freak.'

'Don't want what?' asked Bonner as he sidestepped some lengths of piping.

'That new girl Rosa. She had a weird one. She said he felt like someone who didn't come from anywhere. And she thought he was gonna suffocate her. She had a bad cold, see, and he put this stuff on her face. I mean, it could have been acid. But it wasn't. Because whatever it was melted and her cold was completely gone. In seconds. It was like magic, she said.'

Bonner came to a halt on the stairs. Jace turned to look at him.

'What's wrong?' she asked.

There were cheers from the onlookers as Jace led Bonner out from the wreckage of what was left of Dunstall & Sons' fine old red brick building. Jace clasped her hands together and raised them in a winner's salute. She did a twirl. She seemed to be her old self again and the fun was back in her face.

'Pack up all my cares and woe,

Here I go, singing low,
'Bye 'bye blackbird…'

The Dunstall & Sons' motor coaches hadn't even left Gate Town but those on the second coach were determined to sing. Traffic had been reduced to a crawl because of a broken down cement mixer lorry up ahead, but this had failed to dampen the spirits of the holidaymakers.

'Where somebody waits for me,
Sugar's sweet, so is she,
'Bye 'bye blackbird…'

11

A large staff car from Charnham Cross, followed by a chunky SUV, drove along Chain Lane and swung into the street where Rosa lived. Pierce was driving the staff car. Bonner sat beside him. Parking was limited in the narrow street but that was no problem. The vehicles simply double-parked with hazard lights flashing and any poor sod wishing to pull out or get by would just have to fucking wait.

Neighbours peered from windows and doorways and small kids watched from the roadside as Pierce opened the rear door of the staff car for Mrs. O'Day. She climbed from the car with an air of visiting royalty doing some slumming, while Allie and a colleague, wearing protective clothing, hoisted their kit from the SUV.

Rosa had not long got out of bed and was in the bathroom when her bewildered nan let Mrs. O'Day and her team into the house. At first the frail old lady thought it must be to do with the unpaid gas bill or the rent that was overdue, or both. But when Rosa appeared in the kitchen and the questioning started she realised that her grandchild was in trouble again and she began to cry. Rosa couldn't handle this. She shoved her nan into the lean-to scullery and ordered her to fucking stay there.

Having been told where the incident with the strange punter had taken place, Allie and her colleague began to take the front room apart.

Bonner had also been given orders. Mrs. O'Day had told him to stay in the hallway and observe and listen while she and Pierce questioned Rosa because, in her words, 'he was a bit too close to it all.' But then, as he watched and listened he realised that he couldn't have helped much anyway. Because it wasn't as if Rosa was stubborn or was attempting to hide the truth. She was just plain thick.

She said she did not know the name of the man and had never seen him before. She had no idea what he had poured on to her face. She only remembered being scared. She told her questioners that she couldn't find any traces of the mysterious substance the next day. It had just disappeared. And, no, she had not seen the man since. Neither had he given her any information about himself except that he said he came from a long way away. She couldn't recall him having a discernable accent but agreed that she could give some sort of description of the man but not much of one because she wasn't feeling well at the time.

'On October the seventeenth last year,' said Pierce, 'you told Prior Street police that you'd been mugged on your way to the local corner shop.'

'I was.'

'At half past one in the morning?'

'I'd forgotten it was that late.'

'And you were cautioned for wasting police time.'

'Was I?'

'You were also cautioned on the second of January this year for reporting an attempted rape that never took place.'

'Only 'cause the bastards wouldn't believe me,' protested Rosa. 'Anyway, I didn't make no complaint this time, did I? You come to me. I didn't come to you.'

The old lady began crying once more. Rosa shouted at her, 'Just shut the fuck up will you?' She then turned angrily on Bonner in the hallway. She pointed a finger at him. 'Did Jace tell you about all this? A fine fucking friend she is. She wouldn't come out with me that night and she knew I wasn't well. I could have been bloody killed.'

Allie appeared in the hallway. 'We'll run some tests on the bedding and that, Ma'am,' she said. She then indicated Rosa. 'And our M.O. will need to take a look at her just in case.'

'Does this mean you've found no evidence?'

'That's right, Ma'am.'

Mrs. O'Day walked from the room. She said nothing to Bonner, nor did she look at him as he moved along the hallway to open the front door for her.

12

It was three days since the visit to Rosa's house, and Bonner was doing a bit of Christmas shopping in the high street. He'd bought some colourful Indian silk scarves for Jace. And he was tempted, just for fun, to buy his wife a walking stick, which he would then wrap some tinsel around. But he thought better of it because he doubted if Lesley would see the joke. So he settled for something sensible, a lily of the valley toilet gift set and a bath towel.

When he returned to Charnham Cross he met Allie in the administration block. She informed him that so far there was still no evidence as a result of the visit to Rosa's place. Not even a stain, apart from those of the occupiers.

'Maybe there's only ever been four downtimers, Sir,' said Allie as they walked on together. 'One's dead. We've got the other three. Maybe that's it.'

Cliff Talbot was a deadbeat and a piss artist. But he wasn't troublesome. Although he needed the drink and relied upon the perpetual topping up process, he was never nasty with it. It was something he could deal with in his own muddled way. So whenever he felt really bad and sensed that he could be a nuisance to others, he somehow managed to get himself home to his DSS bedsit where he could be a nuisance to just himself and the old MFI wardrobe in his room, which he would always piss in if he couldn't make it down the stairs to the communal loo on the landing. The wardrobe stank, but then so did everything else about Talbot's room and indeed his life, so it didn't really matter.

Only two pieces of tat ever decorated the walls of Talbot's bedsit. One was a small cheap crucifix and the other was a fairly well-worn religious postcard. The picture on the postcard depicted Jesus raising the widow's son. It was a badly painted picture with a cascade of rainbow coloured lights emanating from the Lord's hands as he performed his miracle.

Talbot looked and felt a lot older than his sixty-three years. But right now, as he made his way to Mrs. Pomfret's betting shop in Chain Lane he felt that a change was going to come. Recently he had witnessed something that had haunted him, therefore the postcard had been taken down from the wall and now stayed safely in his jacket inside pocket. As a long lapsed churchgoer, and with Christmas imminent, Clifford Talbot had now made up his mind to return to God. Because at last he knew that God was for real. And he was all set to put a bet on it.

Bonner found Mrs. O'Day in the improvised mortuary. The body of Joseph Valentine now lay on the dissection table and Mrs. O'Day was watching as the pathologist and a mortuary assistant carefully flayed lengths of the check patterned skin from the downtimer's body.

'Allie's had no luck with the girl so far,' said Bonner.

'And the M.O.?' asked Mrs. O'Day.

'The same.'

Mrs. O'Day continued to watch the grisly proceedings. She then moved closer to the mortuary table.

'You thought there was a downtimer on the loose,' she said. 'But you were wrong.'

'A man supposedly in possession of an unknown healing agent?' said Bonner. 'We had to follow it up.'

'Mr. Andrews,' said Mrs. O'Day as she reached for some latex gloves. 'He discovered an unknown healing agent but nobody locked him up.'

Bonner was baffled. 'Who?'

'He invented liver salts.'

The pathologist and his assistant grinned at this. Then, before Bonner could respond, Mrs. O'Day pointed at the dead downtimer. 'Did he have an unknown healing agent? If he did, it didn't do him much good, did it?' She pulled on the latex gloves. 'That little slag was having us on.'

Bonner decided not to answer. It was the same old issue. His private life. There were times when he thought that if Mrs. O'Day had her own way all those who worked for her would not have lives of their own after hours.

Mrs. O'Day reached into a waste receptacle for a strip of bloodied, discarded skin. So that no liquid could drip on to her business suit, she held the strip of skin well away from her as she carried it to a nearby window. Bonner followed her.

'It's the company you keep, Sol,' said Mrs. O'Day in a lowered voice. She held the strip of skin up to the light. 'I told you once, don't fuck up on me. And don't fuck up on yourself. Because these little tarts of yours…'

'They're not my little tarts...'

'They tell lies. They make things up. It's part of their job. Part of their game. You know it is. They keep the punters happy by telling most of the poor sad bastards that they're the best ever. So what about you? How do they keep you happy?'

Bonner wasn't going to be drawn. He decided to shut her up by changing the subject. He indicated the strip of skin that Mrs. O'Day was studying. He turned his head away from the foul smell.

'So what are you going to do with that?'

'Oh, I dunno,' said Mrs. O'Day. 'I might spray it green. Stick some berries on it. Hang it on the front door for Christmas.'

Bonner was amused by this. But he wasn't going to give Mrs. O'Day the benefit of a smile.

13

On Christmas Eve morning Lesley, dressed in her no-nonsense dressing gown and slippers, was cooking Bonner's breakfast. Christmas cards were on display and the lamp shades and picture frames had been hung with tinsel. Bonner watched Lesley as she busied herself at the cooker. He remembered that back in those heady, early marriage days he would have bought her some frilly underwear as a saucy Chrizzy present. But not any more. Those days were long gone. Although he knew that they didn't have to be, considering that there were one or two very sexy forty-two year olds living locally that he'd love to see in suspender belt and stockings.

'Did I tell you we're having Barry and Anne here as usual for Christmas dinner?'

Bonner was dreading the thought of yet another

visit from his brother-in-law. 'Yes, you did, love. How could I forget?'

'I was going to ask Hazel and Jim again as well.' Lesley set Bonner's plate of breakfast down on the table. 'But I thought better of it.'

Although they could bore the arse off a camel as far as Bonner was concerned, he'd prefer to talk to Mr. and Mrs. Deadly Dull from across the street any day.

'You see, I'm getting too old to cook for too many people. I was telling them at the WI. My legs aren't up to it these days.'

Bonner muttered a silent oath to himself as he picked up his knife and fork. Maybe the walking stick wasn't such a bad idea after all, he thought.

A few days ago, while working outside at Charnham Cross, David Doughty had stopped to watch a Christmas tree being delivered. A real one. It was on its way to being set up in the canteen and Doughty wished he could have reached out to smell it, to touch it and to feel its needles. Then two days later he was given the job of cutting foliage for decorations and experienced the joy of gathering freshly cut sprigs of berry-laden holly, mistletoe and spruce. And as he worked he felt sad for the times yet to come when almost all such things in their natural state would be rare and hardly ever seen.

Doughty had been told that strict security meant there were no festivities planned for the three inmates. For them, it would be life as normal, if one could call it normal. But he had been promised a Christmas dinner in his room. And he would even be allowed a glass of wine. He then found himself wondering how the woman and the little girl would spend the yuletide. Although Christmas in his own time period had become less of an event, to him it seemed sad that a child should be kept in confinement at such a time of the year.

During his gardening work at the camp Doughty had often looked for a possible escape route. But there were none within the secure unit. And the guards were always watching. Also, where would he go if he did manage to escape? He would want to find his beloved wife, of course, which meant he would be caught again.

When he had first arrived in this time period he had weighed up the pros and cons of another form of escape, a way back to his own time if he found himself in danger. Before the journey began he was instructed on what to do should that necessity arise. He was to locate the donor site then try it. Try to get back. But he had been warned it was not always a certainty at the first or even the second attempt. Therefore one would have to keep on trying, which he thought would be difficult and highly suspicious should anyone be watching.

Of course, those who had sent him back were unaware that he had no wish to return should the outcome be favourable, which indeed it was once he had met Annette. And, for all its faults, he had grown to like this time on Earth. It suited him. He thought about his wife and wondered how she would be spending the festive season.

Annette was in fact doing OK. As a schoolgirl she had always possessed a good singing voice and was a member of the school choir. And even after all these years she could more or less still hold a note. So while she had been recovering from the hurt and the pain caused by the man who had supposedly used her and lied to her, she had joined a local church choir. But now someone had taken an interest in her. It was the church organist. Whilst he hadn't exactly approached her as yet, she felt it was on the cards. And those fleeting glances during choir practice for the carol concert gave her a bit of a thrill.

The organist was a nondescript man who wore colourless clothes and cold, steely glasses. But

Annette found him reasonably good looking on certain days, if not every day, depending upon her mood. At least he's not a bigamist and an alien, she told herself.

John Pierce was definitely not a Christmas person. And he considered himself lucky not to have to worry about buying presents and cards. Or receiving them. He could even remember trying to avoid Christmas when, as a child, he was living in an orphanage. He hated the institution's stupid games and the cheap and useless Christmas toys. He also hated mixing with the other kids. But then, Pierce had been a loner from the start because he chose to be that way. He had been put into care at a very early age, so there was little he could recall about his parents except that they had big faces and seemed to smell of fish.

Going downstairs to the shop on Christmas Eve to collect his milk and newspaper, Pierce was confronted by the Choudhury family. Their shop was overdressed with gaudy Christmas decorations, and Mrs. Choudhury, on behalf of the family, insisted that their Mister Pierce must dine with them on Christmas day and no excuses. Although it was the last thing Pierce wanted to do, saying no in front of all these expectant faces was obviously out of the question, and the family gave football supporter style whoops and cheers when he accepted the offer.

As Pierce selected a pasty from the hot food cabinet, Mr. Choudhury explained to him that although all members of his family were strict Muslims, they liked the Christian celebrations, and he in particular was fond of the odd glass or two of wine.

'It also means I've got a foot in both camps,' he said, enjoying his own joke. 'Because I intend to get to Heaven even if it kills me.'

On his way to see Jace, Bonner called in at Mrs. Pomfret's betting shop. He was not really a gambling man, and he disliked races like the Grand National because he felt sorry for the horses. But he did like a flutter once a year on one of the Boxing Day meetings.

The betting shop was busy, so Bonner had to queue and wait until Mrs. Pomfret eventually eased her huge frame along the counter to serve him. She was wearing a print dress that made her look like a sofa.

'I've dealt with some crazy people in my time, Sol,' she said as Bonner placed his bet. 'Cliff Talbot. D'you know him?'

'No.'

'Local pisshead. He's put all his savings on what he reckons is a certainty. I told him to forget it and keep his money. But he insisted. 'I even gave him a hundred to one just for the hell of it.'

'So how much is all his savings?'

'The magnificent sum of twenty-three quid.'

'And this certainty?'

'He reckons God is alive and well. Because he can prove it. He's seen him.'

'Where?'

'Would you believe here in Gate Town?'

Bonner grinned as he paid for his bet.

The half net curtains had been removed from one of the downstairs windows of Raymond and Sylvia Pearson's B&B in order to accommodate a Christmas tree. Theirs was the only house in Princess Mary Road to have a tree because right now it was the only house that remained occupied. Three of their four remaining neighbours had given up the struggle with the council and sold out for a rubbish sum. And the fourth, an elderly woman, had escaped to spend Christmas and the New Year with her grown up children.

Just lately the road resembled a war zone with some of the empty houses starting to be demolished, and lorries and rubble and dumper trucks all over the place. And the dust. Always the dust. Sylvia found herself fighting to keep the dust at bay inside the B&B with the help of her dusters and spray polish. But she felt it was a never-ending battle.

On odd occasions, when she was cleaning the outside of the downstairs front windows, construction workers would give derisory wolf-whistles, despite her age, presumably because she was the only female to be seen. And Sylvia hated it when that happened. She felt she was being laughed at. Raymond said he hadn't really noticed the dust that much and maybe she was imagining things, but Sylvia disagreed with him so fiercely and so suddenly that he was obliged to agree with her.

Their Christmas tree was not that big and it was plastic, but it had coloured lights that flickered. It stood on a small table at the window. Looking on the bright side, Sylvia was convinced that the tree and their decorations had cheered things up. And they were lucky to have a paying guest for Christmas.

Sylvia had mentioned the dust to Mr. Silks but he wasn't particularly bothered about it. Although he had told her that wherever he stayed he preferred to tidy his own room. It was a habit of his. He would be delighted to put his bed linen out when it was due for changing, but if he could borrow the necessary cleaning items whenever he felt he needed them, he would be happy with that. Sylvia wasn't that pleased with the idea, but she was prepared to go along with it for the sake of the money it brought in, and because she found him to be an interesting if slightly mysterious man.

While the man in question was reading the Gate Town Gazette that Raymond had driven off to fetch for him, Sylvia chatted about this and that as she pointlessly tidied the dining room. She then asked Shad if Gate Town was going to be suitable for his line of work.

'Yes, I think it will be,' said Shad.

Sylvia was pleased. 'That's good.' She indicated Raymond who had entered the room. 'Of course, Raymond was in show business once. But he didn't last long. People didn't get on with him.'

'Only because there was too much back stabbing,' said Raymond huffily. 'Anyway, it was only am-dram.'

Shad looked up from the newspaper. 'Only what?'

Raymond was a little surprised that their Mr. Silks the illusionist had not heard the expression.

'Amateur dramatics.'

'Oh, of course,' said Shad and returned to the paper.

'And do you have any engagements over the holiday period?' asked Sylvia.

'No,' said Shad with a smile. 'I've nothing booked. Then again, something could always turn up at the last minute.'

If Eve Palmer and David Doughty had ever had a chance to know each other in their own time period, it is doubtful that she would have shared his romantic interest in days of old. The western world in their period was indeed more clinical and more controlled but at least its growth in population had long been curtailed and there was very little disease. Apart from a few rare exceptions, and due to the advances in biotechnological functional foods, what would once have been described as fresh food was a thing of the past. And this had helped to eliminate most of the said diseases that still existed in the few remaining underdeveloped parts of the world.

And, at that time in the future, Eve and others like her cared little about Christmas and all its trappings. Only a scaled-down version of it remained and was celebrated more as a novelty than as an event. Reindeers and robins and suchlike, seen on old pieces of correspondence in museums, were regarded as quaint. There was snow at both poles but nowhere else. That had also been controlled, more by accident than design, in the same way that winter had been reduced.

For Eve, the thought of microbe infested creatures roasted and served up as a ceremonial feast, was both idiotic and barbaric. Yet here she was back in time, having to suffer the indignity of a tawdry pagan ritual. But she was determined that however much Cara's eyes lit up at the decorations that had been hung up around Charnham Cross, and the promise of presents by nurse Claire, she would not allow Mrs. O'Day and her acolytes to get at the truth through her child.

Kenneth the forensic scientist, better known as Fuckhead Ken by his fellow workers, had managed to avoid his laboratory's annual Christmas Eve lunchtime party. He went to the Gantry instead, hoping to see Allie, the woman of his dreams. But she wasn't there. The pub was full of office workers and manual workers happily winding down for the holiday. He ordered half a pint and retreated to a corner to drink it.

As the jolly, happy banter and laughter went on

all around him, Kenneth remembered when he had last seen Allie in the pub, looking stunning in her best office clothes. And he remembered talking to ex sergeant, now inspector, Bonner. Kenneth also recalled not being entirely honest when Bonner had asked him if his team had got any further with the investigation into the murder of the local schoolgirl.

Kenneth was not liked at work. As a result of this he was the object of much piss-taking. He had no proper defence against this because he had no friends, so he responded by being snide and sneery and sarcastic, which made things worse for him, given that he was disliked in the first place because he was a precisionist who worked diligently. This meant he occasionally showed up colleagues who were less conscientious.

But, above all, if some part of Kenneth's investigative work worried him he would never let it go. And it was true that his group, working as forensic provider for the Major Crime Unit, had still made no real headway into the schoolgirl's death.

Yet Kenneth believed he himself may have stumbled upon something during the investigation, but it was something that needed further examinations on his part before informing his superiors. He was also worried about being ridiculed as usual by his colleagues should his findings prove wrong. In the meantime, his curiosity about what he may have discovered still nagged at him. And he felt it was a pity about Christmas. That would get in his way.

The afternoon had remained cold, but only driving rain would prevent Cara from visiting her very own private place, the 'Happy Times' activity centre that had been built for her and her alone. And here she was, wearing a warm woollen hat, scarf and mittens, swinging happily on a swing. Nurse Claire was in attendance and Eve was also there, arms folded and suffering in silence in the cold air, and not prepared to engage in conversation while she waited for the recreational session to finish.

As Clair moved to help Cara from the swing, Eve noticed David Doughty on the other side of the chain link fence at the far end of the compound. He was busy clearing some old dead leaves. His guards were at some distance from him. Eve looked around her and saw that her female guards were turned away and chatting to each other outside the compound gate. At that moment Cara had climbed the tower to get to the top of the slide and she had dropped her mittens in the process. As

Claire moved to pick up the mittens, Eve acted on impulse and ran quickly towards the far end of the compound.

Doughty looked up and saw Eve hurrying towards him. From somewhere, guards could be heard shouting. Eve reached the fence. She grabbed at the wire mesh.

'Do you know anything?' she asked. 'Has something gone wrong?

Then, before Doughty could reply, the guards had reached Eve. One of them took her by the arm and spoke quietly yet firmly, like a nurse dealing with a difficult patient.

'All right, Eve. That'll do.'

Eve let go of the fence. She turned slowly. She saw Cara watching her from the top of the 'Happy Times' tower.

Jace knew how to dress a Christmas tree. This year, as usual, she had bought a real one of medium size. But no cheap tinsel or dangling ornaments for her. Not on her tree. Her tree lights were exquisite. They were small glass candles with clear white bulbs set in silver-finish holders. And the tree branches had been decorated with tiny bows and star shapes, of all colours and textures, made from what seemed like dozens and dozens of pieces of cloth. The tree seemed to have taken over the small living room.

Bonner sat at a table by the window. He had a mug of coffee, and on the table top were some shop-bought mince pies on a plate. Beside them was a clumsily wrapped gift package containing the scarves he had bought for her. He watched Jace as she threaded the last of some lengths of ribbons amongst the cloth shapes and the glass candles. She then got to her feet and moved to the table. She picked up the wrapped present. She read the little card that was clumsily attached to it.

''From me to you'. Is that all?'

'There's kisses on it.'

'Only two of 'em.' She carried the package to the tree. 'Anyway, thanks.' She placed the package down under the tree. It was the only present there. She then moved to a drawer and removed a perfectly wrapped present. She carried it to the table and handed it to Bonner.

'For me?' said Bonner in mock surprise. 'You shouldn't have.'

'No, I shouldn't have, you bastard.' Jace sat down at the table. 'You don't deserve it.' She reached for her tobacco tin and proceeded to make a roll-up. 'Am I seeing you over Christmas?'

'Of course.'

'When?'

'Well, tomorrow's tricky.'

'That's all right. I'm going to Fran's for some lunch and a booze up. Some of the girls are going.'

'Will Rosa be there?'

'No. She's got her nan to worry about.'

'Does her imagination always run away with her? Does she always tell fucking lies?'

'She wasn't telling lies. Not this time. I'm sure of it.'

'Why are you sure of it?'

'Because what she was saying about that fella was so weird. And Rosa never does weird. She does ordinary and she does scary and she does nasty. But she never does weird.'

Bonner thought about this as he looked out of the window at cold Ferry Lane in the grey afternoon light. The pneumatic drills had now stopped working for the Christmas break.

'Hey!'

Bonner turned his head to find Jace tapping the small card that was attached to the present she had given him.

'Never mind about two poxy kisses. It's got 'With Love' on there.'

'Yeah. I saw it.'

Jace nibbled at a mince pie as she smoked her roll-up. 'And I really want to see you for Christmas,

Sol.'

'Don't worry. You will.'

'When?' she insisted.

'Boxing Day. I'll be able to get away Boxing Day. I'll sort it.'

'Good.' She paused for a moment then spoke honestly and without a hint of sentiment, as if stating a fact. 'Because I do love you a bit, Sol. Just a bit.'

'I should hope so.'

'Well, it'd be fucking stupid if I didn't after all this time, wouldn't it?' She paused once more, in thought, as she smoked. 'I was thinking, if I give up what I'm doing I could go back to waitressing.'

'Good idea,' said Bonner.

'Not much money in it, though.'

'But at least it's safe.'

'Yeah,' Jace agreed. 'And maybe I wouldn't have any more of them moods. No more deadness. Could we be together someday? I mean properly together?'

Bonner was unable to answer the question as he would have wished. There were too many things in the way at the moment. Too many problems to solve. 'Someday maybe, yes,' he managed. 'But the time isn't right yet.'

'And would you look after me?'

'Of course I would.'

Jace was satisfied with this. She set the half smoked roll-up down in an ashtray and moved back to the tree. She crawled on hands and knees to switch on a wall socket. The tree burst into life as the lights came on.

'Yay!' she cried and clapped her hands. For Bonner at that moment she seemed even more like a child. And he felt almost paternal towards her as she got to her feet and reached for a small camera. She crouched down, aimed the camera at the tree and took a picture. The camera flashed.

Bonner was reminded of something as the camera continued to click and flash. 'Picture, light, small ghost,' he said aloud to himself. 'It doesn't make sense.'

Jace moved to take a shot from another angle. 'What doesn't?'

'Oh, it's something a little kid said.'

'Well, little kids never make sense.'

Bonner continued to think aloud. 'Because if the ghost is the image, then it should be the other way round when a photo's taken, shouldn't it? Image, light, picture.'

'If you say so,' said Jace.

Bonner looked at his watch. He got up from his chair. 'Better go,' he said. He picked up his present from her and handed it to Jace. 'I can't take this with me.'

'I know.' She took the package from him. 'We'll open these on Boxing Day. Together.'

'Yeah,' said Bonner. 'We'll have a good piss-up.'

'And a good cuddle. I need that.' Jace placed the package under the tree beside her present.

As Bonner reached for his overcoat he took another look out of the window at Ferry Lane in the fading light.

On that hot summer's day in 1961 the traffic on the link road was moving at long last.

'Oh, we ain't got a barrel of money,

Maybe we're ragged and funny,

But we'll travel along, singing a song, side by side…'

Progress was slow, but at least the wheels were turning as the long line of vehicles edged its way towards the bypass. And the Dunstall & Sons' day trippers on the second coach were still in good cheer.

'Oh, we don't know what's coming tomorrow,

Maybe it's trouble and sorrow,

But we'll travel the road, sharing our load, side by side…'

Fat Mary from sales was the wrong shape

and the wrong age to pull up her skirt and begin dancing in the aisle. It caused a great deal of laughter and some shouts of, 'Get 'em off!' along with even louder shouts of, 'No, keep 'em on!'

Mr. Michael felt a little uncomfortable with the ribaldry. He looked quickly in Karen's direction and was relieved to see that she was amused by the antics, and her little boy was laughing and clapping his hands. Karen then turned her head to look at Mr. Michael and smile another warm smile, and at that moment in time he felt he must be the happiest person on the coach. He even joined in with the song.

'Through all kinds of weather,

What if the skies should fall?

As long as we're together, it doesn't matter at all…'

Seeing a gap, the first coach eased onto the nearside lane of the bypass. In an attempt to keep up with the leader, the second coach pulled out in a hurry. A fully laden car-transporter, running late and travelling at speed, could not stop in time. It clipped the offside of the second coach, forcing it to career down a short embankment, where, with an almighty screeching, graunching sound and a cascade of broken glass and metal, its front nearside was crushed against a concrete support column.

14

It was early evening and quite dark in Princess Mary Road. The street lamps had been switched off some time ago as part of the dismantling of the area, but Raymond and Sylvia's Christmas tree shone brightly in the front window of the B&B.

Inside the house, Sylvia was hoping that their paying guest might join them for a Christmas Eve drink. Although she knew that he liked to go out walking at night, sometimes until late, even though she couldn't understand why, she had nevertheless invited him. But she had insisted it was an informal invitation and he only need accept if he wanted some company.

So she had done her best to make their lounge look festive and cosy. She had baked home-made cheese twists and mince pies, and there were glasses and a bottle of medium dry sherry on the table. Raymond had been told to expect his supper later, and was ordered to keep his shoes on and not to slouch around in slippers as he usually did every evening after they'd finished their chores.

As they waited they heard the sound of footsteps on the stairs. In anticipation, Sylvia did some quick, last moment fussing with the goodies on the table. There was then the sound of the front door being opened and closed. The couple turned to look in the direction of the hallway.

'Must be having one of his walks,' said Raymond.

Sylvia did not answer. For some extraordinary reason she found herself feeling hurt and angry. It was as though she had been rejected. Or stood up, even. And this last thought made her feel foolish. So much so, that she railed at Raymond as he helped himself to a couple of cheese twists.

David Doughty had finished his gardening work for the Christmas break and he was sorry. Charnham Cross had no formal gardens and what had supposedly passed as an attempt at landscaping could not be described as attractive. But Doughty enjoyed the job of looking after what there was of it. He had even managed to make modest improvements to the area.

Of course there was no appreciation for his dedicated work from Mrs. O'Day and those close to her, and he didn't expect any, but the eldest of his guards, a keen home gardener, had rewarded him with a cheap, simple Christmas card. It was his only card and it stood on the small table in his confinement quarters. Sellotaped to the wall beneath the bulkhead light were a few strands of colourful paper chains. These had been provided voluntarily by the catering staff.

It was obvious to Doughty that decorations made of metal or synthetic materials had been disallowed in case he tried to harm himself. He had wanted to collect some cut sprigs of ivy and holly to bring cheer to his surroundings, but this had evidently been denied for the same reason. Still, he didn't really mind. To him the paper chains were quite old fashioned. As was the simple card. And he approved of that. He'd had enough of the almost total use of synthetics in his own world.

He thought about the woman who had called out to him in the compound. She was obviously involved in the same project that had sent him here, but why had she brought a child back with her?

Doughty had never told Annette what his true occupation was. He was sure she wouldn't have understood. And it was important in those early days of getting to know her and eventually loving her, that she should not know where he came from. He was worried that that may have frightened her. And he didn't want to lose her. So he had planned on telling her the truth once they had been married for some length of time. But, sadly, that day had never come.

From outside there was the sound of the main door being unlocked and opened, then the clatter of a metal trolley on the iron gantry. Doughty's evening meal was arriving.

Like most buildings of worship, the interior of Gate Town's Holy Trinity church was not the warmest place to be on a cold winter's evening. But as the congregation arrived for the carol concert the Reverend Phipps assured them that once everyone was giving good voice and enjoying themselves to the full, things would quickly warm up, and there would be mince pies and mulled wine for all at the end of the service.

Annette was with the other choir members. To her, the interior of the church looked splendid with the glow of candles, the decorated wreaths and garlands and the colourful baby Jesus crib that had been made and bedecked by the local children. And she was pleased to notice that even Neville the organist seemed less ashen-looking in this light as he peeped over his music sheet and gave her a little smile.

There were strange coats and scarves hanging up in the hallway as Bonner opened his front door and stumbled over a wheeled walking frame. Badly in need of a large scotch, he found Lesley entertaining four members of her W.I. group at the kitchen table. They were sipping homemade wine and making notes for their forthcoming New Year's Eve meeting-cum-party.

Bonner didn't wish to feel unkind, but, apart from Lesley, he thought they all looked as though they had one foot in the grave. He remembered Lesley telling him that this particular branch of the W.I. couldn't attract younger women. Now he could understand why. Nevertheless, the visitors were happy and chatty and they urged Bonner to sample some of the elderflower wine, made by Mavis, the owner of the walking frame. He took a swig and praised it to high heaven, even though it tasted like penetrating oil. He then made an excuse and escaped to the living room.

Later that evening, after the W.I. gang had toddled off on their separate ways and Lesley had gone to bed, Bonner sat thinking about it all. He was on his third large scotch and he wished himself a happy fucking Christmas and wondered what had happened to his life. The prospect of living with Jace appealed to him. But there was Lesley to consider. He decided that if she'd bothered to make the effort she could still be OK, could still look and think and talk like a forty-two year old woman. But that now seemed beyond her.

In other words it was too late. These well-meaning but sad old dears, with their tight, white, cauliflower-head perms and their elderflower-piss wine had got her. It was like those old horror films, he thought, when the heroine gets ensnared by some wicked cult, like devil worshippers or, in the more salacious movies, evil swingers, until the victim is eventually saved in the nick of time by the hero. Except this was different. His loving wife had been taken over by the crumblies. And, as far as he could see, rescue was out of the question and the search had been called off.

Even though her Mr. Silks was not at home, Sylvia moved quietly up the stairs of the B&B to the door of his room. When he first arrived he had asked for a key to the room, which she had agreed to with a certain amount of reluctance. But then she had a master key which she now used to unlock the door.

She entered just as quietly and switched on the light. The room was neat and tidy, mainly because Mr. Silks did not have enough possessions to clutter up a small room. Sylvia had once mentioned this to him in a friendly way and he had told her that he was expecting some luggage to be sent on to him. Yet that was weeks ago and so far nothing had arrived.

Sylvia wasn't quite sure what she was looking for, but because she had been upset by the man's lack of interest in her offer, she was somehow wondering if he'd perhaps had a last minute invitation to a more important do, or perhaps there had been a problem at some theatrical venue somewhere and he had been summoned as a last-minute replacement. She then remembered that she had never known him to receive mail or telephone calls. And, as far as she knew, he did not possess a mobile phone. If he did she had never seen it or heard it ring.

Being so preoccupied with her guest, she also saw this as an opportunity to find out just a little more about him, if that were possible.

She opened the wardrobe door and saw three or four shirts on hangers. She then opened the top drawer of a chest of drawers and saw underpants and socks. The bottom drawer contained nothing more than a local street map, magazines, assorted envelopes, folders and a couple of back copies of the Gate Town Gazette. Finding nothing that she considered untoward, she closed the drawer, opened the door and switched off the light.

Then, as she turned to close the door behind her, she saw just the faintest glow of light from the edge of the bottom drawer. It flickered just once, and then stopped. Sylvia switched the light back on. She moved to the drawer and opened it. She then realised that she must have imagined things because there was still nothing inside except magazines, envelopes and papers.

As she moved back down the stairs, Sylvia was worried that the flicker of light could have heralded the start of one of her migraine attacks.

Raymond was waiting for her at the foot of the stairs. 'Can we eat now?' he asked.

'Yes. Go on,' Sylvia shrieked at him. 'Don't worry about me. Just stuff your greedy face.'

Although he had made up his mind to steer clear of the Cat in the Cradle for a while, Shad had decided on giving the pub another visit. He was in need of pleasure and surely tonight of all nights would be when the very young ladies, with or without colds, were out in force. He had spent a fruitless hour or so investigating the Chain Lane area but the only females there were too old for him and were mostly working in pairs or plying their trade within sight of each other.

So the Cat in the Cradle it had to be. But once again he was disappointed. The pub was busy, but, being Christmas Eve it was mostly made up of families, along with assorted groups of boisterous, brassy women in their twenties, let loose from the stores and the workshops and the offices for the Christmas holiday. And it was noisy with trashy Christmas songs blaring from speakers and everyone trying to be heard by shouting over each other.

Shad managed to make his way to the bar counter through this too loud, too jolly, too happy free-for-all. Once there he had to wait his turn to be served. And, as he looked around him, he realised that he was probably the only person in the pub without a companion. Oh, where oh where, he asked himself, is there a lost and lonely little mystery of a girl waiting for someone like me to buy her a drink and introduce her to some real entertainment?

Luckily for Shad, tonight's customers were not the Cat in the Cradle's usual clientele, and the landlord and his wife were not on duty, neither was the young barmaid, therefore there was no-one likely to ask him to perform another of his tricks.

But Shad was not the only lone person in the pub. He was being watched, with a look of awe, by a small, shabby, fairly intoxicated individual who was doing his best not to be jostled and overwhelmed by the high-spirited crowd.

Cliff Talbot had never forgotten that evening not long ago when he had seen a miracle performed in this very pub. The raising, not of the dead, but of the living – a girl in a chair. To his befuddled mind, whether he'd been drunk or sober, he had seen God that night. Or Jesus. Or maybe both acting as one. Either way, he was convinced he had witnessed the second coming. That was why he had put a bet on it.

God had not put in an appearance since that night, and whenever Talbot had asked the bar staff if they'd seen him, they didn't know what the fuck he was talking about. But now God, or Jesus, was here again on this holiest of nights. Because Talbot had spotted him standing quietly at the bar amidst the noisy, jabbering throng. The believer smiled a drunken, beatific smile and managed to cross himself with difficulty as an order of drinks for some rowdy customers was thrust past his face. He then took the garish postcard from his pocket and held it on high.

'God of love, Father of all,' Talbot said aloud, trying in vain to compete with the barrage of noise. 'The darkness that covered the Earth has given way to the bright dawn of your word…'

Shad had turned his head and noticed a maniacal looking primitive staring at him and mouthing words as it held aloft some sort of picture. Shad therefore decided to leave because he was already tired of the din and the smell of these people. Having finished his drink, he edged his way to the door.

Still praying aloud, Talbot dropped his postcard, scrabbled around on the floor to find it, then struggled his way through a pack of drinkers who were guffawing and braying at some joke, 'Make us a people of this light,' he cried as he fought his way to the door. 'Make us faithful to your Word that we may bring your life to the waiting world…'

Sylvia was washing up and Raymond was wiping as their front door was heard to open and close. Sylvia moved through the kitchen to the partly open hall door to listen. She would be the last to admit it, but secretly she was wishing that Mr. Silks might call to her and then apologise for his absence before explaining that it was an emergency he had

had to deal with. But no. She heard him climb the stairs, then unlock and open the door of his room. The door was then closed behind him.

'That's it,' said Sylvia as she bustled back into the kitchen. 'He certainly won't be invited to Christmas lunch.'

Outside in the dark road with its rubble and dust and scaffolding and skips full of junk, the lights from Sylvia's Christmas tree were shining. Talbot was standing on the opposite pavement. He was watching the B&B. He told himself that he had won his bet. His Saviour was here.

It makes sense, he assured himself, because all those years ago the Son of God arrived not amongst crowds and not in some gleaming palace, but in a lowly stable. And now he has returned to yet another lowly place, this misbegotten road.

Up in his room, Shad was in the process of removing his coat. He stopped and looked around him. He couldn't be sure, but he had the feeling that someone had been in the room. He checked the wardrobe and the chest of drawers but found that nothing appeared to have been disturbed. He then thought he could hear a voice from outside. He moved to the window and peered out. But he could see nothing.

Hidden in the darkness on the other side of the road, Talbot had put his hands together and was looking up at Shad's silhouette in the lighted window. He was praying aloud once more. 'Dear Lord, since you came from Heaven to Earth on that day you forgave our sins and wiped away our guilt...'

A black limo with tinted glass weaved its way along the unlit, bumpy track that led to the gates of Charnham Cross. The car was followed by a matching black Range Rover.

Mrs. O'Day had stayed late at Charnham Cross. Christmas Eve was not for her, so she had taken advantage of the peace and quiet to finish off some paperwork. She was all set to go home when the surprise phone call had come through.

She was waiting as the two dark vehicles drove through the gates and parked outside the administration building. Smartly suited security men emerged from the Range Rover and adopted protective poses as the driver of the diplomatic car opened the car's rear door and the only other occupant climbed from it. He was an immaculately dressed man of late middle age. As he shook Mrs. O'Day's hand he gave her the coldly polite smile of someone who was here simply on business, and nothing more.

With the security men keeping a discreet but ever watchful distance, Mrs. O'Day showed her visitor around the interior of Charnham Cross and explained the state of play. The man was shown the frozen remains of the downtimer, the skin samples and the stored belongings of the inmates. He then watched, via the surveillance cameras, Doughty, Eve and the sleeping Cara. He was particularly interested in the news about the child's eyes and asked for a separate report on this, plus x-ray results, to be sent to him as soon as possible.

Later, in Mrs. O'Day's office, more questions were asked, and existing reports were looked at, into the early hours. So it was almost twenty-to-three on Christmas morning when Mrs. O'Day was at last allowed to say goodnight to her departing visitor and make her way home.

15

Cara was fast asleep in her bed, but Eve was awake at four o'clock on Christmas morning. As she lay there in thought, she remembered being assured that apart from the rare possibility of some risks, all would be well with the project, especially as those who were to follow would assist her. But now she found herself worrying that perhaps Timelight should not have rushed things. But then they had to, she reminded herself. They were under pressure.

By the feeble light of the dimmer bulb, Eve could see the paper chain decorations provided by the catering staff, and the Christmas card and small box of chocolate animals given to Cara by nurse Claire. At first, Eve had been annoyed and wanted these stupid gifts taken away. But Cara had cried so bitterly that Eve allowed them to stay. For the child's sake. Not for hers.

Ever aware of the surveillance camera, Eve eased herself from her bed. She moved to pick up a towel which she had deliberately left draped over Cara's bedside cupboard. The towel was covering the pencil case. In picking up the towel, Eve also gathered up the pencil case. She carried the hidden item to the side of the washroom alcove that was out of range of the camera. Pretending to be using the towel, she slid a piece of fake lining from the pencil case. The double sheeted lining had been fashioned from the red plastic folder she had bought from the Gate Town stationers.

As Eve separated a tiny portion of the two sheets there was a brief jumble of bright, shimmering colours. Although worried that the reflected light might possibly have been detected by the camera, she was relieved to find that what lay inside was still active. That was of vital importance to her. She slipped the lining back inside the pencil case and covered it once more with the towel. Leaving the hidden case in the alcove for now, she returned to her bed.

Despite her late night, Mrs. O'Day was up just before seven a.m. There were no yuletide decorations in her flat. And no festive food in the fridge or the kitchen cupboards. She had received three Christmas cards but they were not on display, nor would they be. They remained in their opened envelopes and lay on the hall table with some bills and some junk mail. She drew back the living room curtains, then, as usual, drank her coffee and smoked a fag as she gazed at the architectural delights of Ferry Lane.

Christmas can go fuck itself, she decided.

Today was one of those days when Mrs. O'Day felt edgy. The edginess, like an illness, always came on suddenly and without warning. When this happened during working hours her colleagues usually kept their distance. Sometimes the bouts of edginess happened for no obvious reason. But she knew what had triggered this one. It was last night's visitor at Charnham Cross. As superiors go he was new to her. And he worried her. His coldness worried her. His upper class politeness was all charm itself. But there was still the chilling coldness.

To take her mind of this, she pottered around doing odd little tasks. She switched on the radio but found nothing to listen to apart from crap Christmas songs and presenters who were determined to be jolly at all costs. So she ran a bath instead and lay in the hot, scented water. This relaxed her a little. But the edginess remained. And the worrying thoughts returned.

Up to now, those who employed her and supposedly trusted her had allowed her to continue with her current assignment without undue interference. In fact, there were times when she felt it seemed like indifference on their part and assumed that this was probably all part of them keeping it quiet and out of the ears and eyes of the public and the press.

But for her, last night's unexpected visit had changed all that. The man had praised her for her efficiency, and he had shown interest in the downtimers and asked about their well-being, especially that of the child. But behind it all was the coldness. And that remained. She sensed that perhaps some kind of decision may have been made, one that she had not been informed of as yet. She then put this down to random paranoia which was something she was particularly good at when she was feeling edgy. It caused her to wonder if the downtiming threat had subsided. And if so, what next? What would the future hold for her?

She immediately dismissed this train of thought because she was fully aware that this really was her paranoia getting ready to have itself a field day and she wasn't prepared to put up with that right now. So she climbed from the bath and got dressed.

Mrs. O'Day never usually drank until the evening. But today she thought she'd make just one small contribution to the Christmas spirit. At exactly nine-fifty-five that morning she had her first gin and tonic of the day.

On the other side of Gate Town, Fuckhead Ken was not happy about Christmas. It meant time away from his forensic work and the possibility of catching sight of Allie. Two years ago his wife had left him for pastures that were new and more sexually fulfilling. He was then stupid enough to sell the house and give her most of the proceeds before returning to live with his elderly, widowed mum and his overweight spinster sister who had never left home.

Their mum wasn't exactly in her dotage because she still had her wits about her. But having both children back under her wing had somehow given her a new lease of life which, at times, was proving to be a little uncomfortable and somewhat creepy for the fully grown up siblings. Kenneth was thirty-seven and his sister was forty-two, but on certain occasions, dear old Mum would see them as small children once more. She would even adopt the sing-song tones that adults use when they are talking down to tiny tots. And, borrowing from her own childhood days, she would insist on a once-a-week Sunday sit down tea, when she would serve up miniature sausage rolls, buttered slices of bread, dishes of tinned fruit salad, and blancmange.

Kenneth had no hobbies. Apart from his obsession with Allie, the only thing that interested him was his work. And right now, with time on his hands, those little nagging doubts about the young girl's murder and the subsequent forensic investigation still worried him. He knew that for his own peace of mind he had to find out more.

At the B&B, Sylvia had got herself into a fine old state. Pretending to have sciatica, she had stayed in bed because she couldn't face serving Mr. Silks his breakfast. She was still hurt by what she considered to be his bad behaviour in dismissing her invitation for a Christmas Eve drink. Yet at the same time she couldn't understand why she felt this way, because she acknowledged that Mr. Silks had every right to live his own life and go about his own business, however unusual that business might be. It made her feel confused.

So it was left to Raymond to serve the man his breakfast and explain that his wife was not very well. He had also been instructed to apologise in advance for not inviting their guest to Christmas lunch, and to say that he and Sylvia always preferred to spend that particular meal alone together because they had first met one Christmas day many years ago, and it was now an established anniversary moment for them. Raymond was not happy about saying this because it was untrue. And he hated telling lies. He also hated having to refer to the proverbial Christmas dinner as Christmas lunch, but Sylvia would not have it any other way, so there was nothing Raymond could do about it. He was therefore relieved that Mr. Silks was in good spirits and even announced that he was perfectly happy with things as they are because he never ate lunch anyway, Christmas or otherwise.

The local weather forecast had got it wrong. They said it would be a clear but chilly day with the possibility of some light showers. But by midday the freezing fog had descended once more on Gate Town.

The fog meant that Lesley's brother and his wife arrived late at the Bonner house. Bonner didn't mind at all and had been hoping that the weather might have put the prick off completely. But no such luck. The man complained that according to the national radio the weather wasn't quite as bad in other parts of the south of England, so he blamed Gate Town itself for what he called local industrial pollution, despite the fact that the factories were closed for the holiday and there was less traffic. It was a load of balls of course, but Bonner wasn't going to tell him so because that would mean having to endure some kind of conversation with the man. So, while Lesley served up a grand feast of roast turkey, roast spuds, roast parsnips, Brussels sprouts, mashed swede, bread sauce and gravy, they had to suffer a lecture on what should have been learned from the horrors of the great London smogs of fifty-two and sixty-two.

In the back room parlour of the Choudhury shop there were no lectures. It was just one noisy, colourful, crazy, sit-down party. Asian music was playing from a sound system in the background and there was loud, happy, non-stop chatter. The first course, which had been part Bangladeshi and part English, had been consumed. Crackers had been pulled and party poppers were being popped, and Mrs. Choudhury and the elder daughters dressed in shiny, beautiful clothes, were serving up desserts.

Pierce was sitting through it all with a slightly bewildered but contented expression on his face.

He was not used to too much noise. Or people. Or colour. Or Christmas. And he normally avoided kindness. But today he was doing OK. No-one was asking him stupid questions. He was just there.

'See what you think of these, Mr. Pierce.' Mrs. Choudhury, looking quite glamorous, was handing him a small glass bowl of syrupy looking round fried objects.

Pierce adjusted the Christmas cracker paper hat that he had been made to wear. He looked suspiciously at the sweet.

'You'll like them,' insisted Mrs. Choudhury

Pierce, who had already eaten more than he was used to, picked up one of the fried balls with a spoon. He bit into it. He was surprised by the taste.

'It's bloody delicious,' he exclaimed. And he meant it.

Right there and then he could have been the man from Del Monte. There was a roar of approval from the entire Choudhury family as Pierce reached for another spoonful. The table was thumped. More party poppers exploded. Mr. Choudhury leant across the table and topped up Pierce's glass.

Neither were there lectures at Raymond and Sylvia's dining table. Or fun. The fog at the window made it seem as though evening had arrived too early. But at least the small Christmas tree was able to brighten up the proceedings even if nothing else could.

The couple ate their meal in silence, with Sylvia occasionally glancing at the door or listening for sounds from upstairs. But there had been no sight of Mr. Silks since breakfast.

'He's got to go,' said Sylvia.

Raymond looked up from his meal. 'What?'

'After New Year's Eve he's got to go. I don't want him here.'

'But he's done nothing wrong.'

Sylvia put down her knife and fork and leaned sharply back in her chair, chin thrust upright. It was a warning to Raymond that if he dared answer back at this moment her sciatica or migraine or some other fake fucking illness would come back with a vengeance. So he shut up and continued with his meal.

'And there's something going on in his room.'

Raymond looked up once more. 'Like what?'

Although evidence of misconduct on their paying guest's part was thin on the ground, Sylvia, in her tortured state, was determined to gather as much of it as she could.

'Something strange,' she said.

But at least paper hats and crackers were also the order of the day at Fuckhead Ken's house. Christmas time meant kiddy time as far as his old mum was concerned, so she had been in her element. At break of day that morning a filled stocking had been quietly hung at the foot of Kenneth's sweaty bed. His sister, who still slept in the same room she grew up in, still snored, and still hung her clothes on the floor, was also the early recipient of a filled stocking by a tip-toeing mum.

There had then been a present opening ceremony at breakfast time, with Kenneth and his sister receiving gifts such as scarves, socks, sweets, jig-saws and small board games. And then it had been the biggie, Christmas dinner with a full roast and the option of jelly and custard to follow for whoever didn't want Christmas pudding. But worse was to come, because, hanging over it all, was the threat of having to sit down as a family to watch the Queen's speech on TV.

'Then what?' Kenneth's sister had managed to mutter to him, as she eased her way from the table to have a pee and a fag. 'I hope she doesn't expect us to play pass the fucking parcel.'

But Kenneth had other thoughts on his mind as his mother poured custard over his portion of Christmas pud.

By the time Mrs. O'Day left home she had downed two more gin and tonics. So she was in a fairly jovial state of mind as she made her way through the fog to the Gantry. She had decided to get out from her flat because the enveloping gloom was beginning to piss her off.

The pub had only opened for the lunchtime session, but it was lively and friendly and busy, with everyone trying to make the most of things before last orders were called. Mrs. O'Day was welcomed by Clumpy Ron and the regulars. Even George the landlord managed to lift his arse off his stool and reach across the bar to shake her hand and wish her a happy Christmas.

'That's on me,' he said as Clumpy Ron served up a gin and tonic.

As the session progressed, Mrs. O'Day was bought a couple more rounds from the regulars, listened to their Christmas day family plans, had to put up with the odd sob story, was told some fairly dirty jokes, told a couple of very dirty ones in return, sang along loudly to snatches of juke box music and found herself having a very enjoyable time.

When George eventually rang last orders, and with the merry throng preparing to return home to loved ones and despised ones and crazy ones,

Mrs. O'Day suddenly felt like sad shit. So instead of going straight home she made up her mind that she was going to get herself a companion for the rest of the afternoon, whether that companion liked the idea or not.

She bought a large round of drinks, then bade her farewells as the door opened and Rosa entered. Despite the cold weather, the youngster was wearing the shortest and flimsiest of skirts. She gave Mrs. O'Day a pantomime look of menace as she moved to the bar.

Mrs. O'Day was amused by the look and by Rosa's outfit. 'You'll catch another cold, sweetheart.'

'Bollocks!' the girl replied.

'Never mind what you had for breakfast,' said Mrs. O'Day as she weaved her way to the door. As she stepped outside she found that the fog had thinned only slightly. A couple of cars passed by with their fog lights on. She lit a fag. She took her mobile from her pocket and dropped it. 'Fuck!' she said as she stooped down to retrieve it.

Bonner was not a wine drinker. It had never appealed to him and it gave him heartburn. So he only drank a glass and a half with his meal. He was waiting for the meal to finish so he could start on the hard stuff.

'As usual, that was wonderful,' said Lesley's sister-in-law. 'You've always been such a good cook.'

'Thank you,' said Lesley. 'But I'm afraid this may be the last Christmas dinner I make. You see, it's such a lot of effort. And I'm not as young as I was.'

Bonner gave a 'Heaven help us' sigh.

'But you're not old, sis,' said her brother through a mouthful of food.

'Oh, I am. I feel it. I feel older every day.' She gave a sad smile. Her brother stopped eating. He looked at his sister with concern. It was the first time Bonner had seen the man showing interest in someone else. It made him seem almost human.

Then Bonner's mobile rang. He mumbled some kind of excuse then got up from the table and went in search of the phone. On this occasion he had left it beside his bed. He picked it up.

'Hello?'

Mrs. O'Day's voice came loud and clear. 'Sol? Where the fuck are you?'

Kenneth's mum was snoring loudly from the comfort of her armchair while the Queen's speech droned on. His sister was taking advantage of the situation by smoking a fag as she watched the TV.

Kenneth took even more advantage by sneaking out of the room, pulling on coat and scarf and creeping out of the house.

As he walked through the murky streets he yet again pondered over the ligature wound on the girl's neck and some shreds of fibre that had been found there. The forensic examination remained inconclusive and so far there were no DNA matches.

Like his colleagues Kenneth was aware of the fact that thousands and thousands of cheap items are imported on a regular basis, as well as dodgy, synthetic fake clothes smuggled in from places like Asia and eastern Europe, so establishing where the fibres had come from was still ongoing. But Kenneth wanted to dig deeper. So he had appropriated some of the tiny threads, or threadlets as he had called them, for further examination. He had analysed one or two and found, like his colleagues, that they were of an unknown synthetic material. A further test on his part revealed that the dye used to colour the fibres was also untraceable. He had then attempted to dissolve one of the specimens but it had remained intact. He had made notes and he was all set to make further tests when Christmas arrived.

A security patrol car, with tinsel attached to its aerial, appeared out of the fog as Kenneth swiped in his controlled access info at his group's laboratory gates. He showed his I.D. and told the security men that he had work to complete despite it being a holiday. They accepted this.

Kenneth entered the empty main building and made his way to the canteen where he switched on the hot drinks vending machine. There were a few tatty decorations as well as wine stained table tops, dirty paper cups and scraps of leftover food from the lab Christmas do, with no cleaners until after the holiday. And no heating.

In the lab itself someone had felt-penned 'shit face' and 'party pooper' on the wall above Kenneth's work area. But he ignored it as he set down his paper cup of coffee and switched on his equipment.

Bonner drove carefully through the gloomy, almost empty streets of Gate Town. Mrs. O'Day sat beside him.

'So where d'you want to go?' he asked.

'Anywhere.' Mrs. O'Day's drink-fuelled feelings of good cheer were beginning to fade somewhat. 'Just drive around.'

'OK.'

'Fucking Christmas. Fuck-all to do.'

'You could have come to my place.'

'Fuck that. If I wanted punishment I could have stayed in and done me ironing.'

Bonner had a quiet chuckle to himself. He would never have invited her anyway. Having taken the phone call, he had told Lesley and his guests that there was an emergency at work and he was needed.

The prick of a brother-in-law had been outraged. 'On Christmas day? What about your wife? What about Lesley?'

Lesley had said nothing. She had simply switched into long-suffering mode before walking into the kitchen and bursting into tears, although she wasn't quite sure why.

Bonner had to manoeuvre the car around a lorry that had lost its way and had stopped in the middle of the road. 'So what did you get for Christmas?' he asked.

'Fuck all,' said Mrs. O'Day. She lit another cigarette. She peered through the car window at the fog. 'Must be somewhere we can get a drink and pretend to be alive.'

'You'll be lucky.'

Bonner came to the conclusion that something was bothering her and it wasn't just Christmas. And he knew too well that it wasn't wise to show concern for Mrs. O'Day's well-being. That brought out the worst in her. So he didn't ask. But then he found he didn't need to.

'I had a visitor last night,' she said as she drew on her fag and continued to peer idly out of the window.

Bonner swerved to avoid a moving cyclist almost hidden by the fog. He glanced at Mrs. O'Day. But that was all she was prepared to say. For now.

On this holiest of days the only suggestion of life in the present-day hell-hole known as Princess Mary Road was still the small Christmas tree in the front window of Raymond and Sylvia's B&B. The tree's coloured lights shone bravely through the fog. Then, above it, from Shad's window, came a sudden burst and swirl of bright, multicoloured lights that flickered busily and seemed to fill the room. It was only for an instant, but in that short time it outshone the Christmas tree and put it to shame.

Sylvia was putting clean crockery away when she heard Shad descending the stairs. She stopped what she was doing. She waited. She then heard the front door open and close. She hurried into the lounge where Raymond was sitting and reading. She moved to the front window and peered between the branches of the Christmas tree. But the fog made it impossible to see anything outside.

'He's gone out again,' she said.

Raymond looked up from his Radio Times. 'Why shouldn't he go out?'

'Because it's Christmas, that's why.' Yet again, Raymond's sensible calmness was beginning to take its toll on Sylvia's nerves. She turned from the window. 'And nothing's open. There's nowhere for him to go. And it'll be dark soon.'

'Maybe he just wants a breath of fresh air.'

'In this weather?' Sylvia almost screeched.

Kenneth's kept his coat and scarf on as he worked. From time to time he warmed his hands over his lit Bunsen burner. He had retrieved his notes and sealed specimen jar containing the threadlets from a safe place, his locked locker.

Having previously tried dissolving one of the minute lengths of fibre in acid without any luck, he decided he would now try burning one. Wearing a magnifier, he unsealed the jar and removed one of the threadlets with tweezers. He attempted to burn the threadlet with the use of the Bunsen burner, but, apart from a slight discolouration, it had stayed intact. He then transferred the threadlet to the plate of a micromanipulator and used a cutter to try to separate the threadlet, but still had no luck.

Kenneth rubbed his hands together vigorously to warm them before making further notes. As he did so he thought he saw a flicker of coloured light from the specimen jar. He turned quickly, but there was nothing to be seen. He assumed it was the reflection from the burner flame.

Wearing the magnifier once more, he reached for the tweezers so that he could carefully pick up the threadlet and return it to the jar. He was then startled to see the length of material, thinner than that of a spider's web, twist and turn of its own volition. It then wrapped itself tightly around one prong of the tweezers before letting go as if it were a coiled spring. At the same time Kenneth thought he saw the tiniest pinpoint of coloured light flash from it for the briefest of moments.

Pleased with his eureka findings, Kenneth no longer felt cold. He felt good. He felt lucky. He would surprise his colleagues and impress his superiors as soon as they returned to work. But right now, if he had the courage, he thought it would be the perfect excuse to share his discovery with a certain other person, despite it being Christmas. He felt that in a strange way the festive season made it quite romantic.

He went into the nearest office and stood by the

phone for a moment or two before deciding to go for it. He then picked up the receiver and nervously tapped in a number.

Fine big Allie, lusted after by many at Charnham Cross, enjoyed doing sod-all at Christmas. She was a Saturday nighter and a birthday celebrator and a New Year's Eve girl and a wedding party lover, providing it wasn't her own wedding. And on those occasions she could live it up and get rat-arsed with the best of them. But not Christmas. It was not for her. Christmas was to be avoided because it smacked too much of the noisy, fault-finding family that she had managed to escape from when she was in her teens.

So she was happy in her cosy flat, with her two contented cats by her side, on this cold, foggy, late afternoon. Dressed in a woolly wrap, she was pigging-out in front of the TV with fluffy slippers on her feet and plenty of chocolates at hand. Pure bliss. Until the phone rang.

Bonner's car drove past the shuttered shops of the high street, then proceeded for another three quarters of a mile before turning into Sutherland Avenue. The avenue and its neighbouring streets were not exactly up-market, because nowhere in Gate Town could really be described as such. It had as much tackiness and litter as the rest of the town, but it was quieter, more sedated than sedate, mainly because most of its residents were at, or well past, retirement age. Bonner reckoned there were more disabled parking bays in and around Sutherland Avenue than anywhere else in town simply because there were more clumpies in residence there.

As they drove through this necropolis for the living, Bonner reckoned he'd just about had enough. He was about to explain to Mrs. O'Day that he ought to get back home. But she was pointing ahead through the windscreen.

'Up there. The Walholme is open. I should have remembered. They usually do it at Christmas.'

Through the fog, Bonner could see lighted windows and an illuminated sign. 'Do what?'

'Entertain the fumble and fart brigade.'

It was just gone four thirty when the Cat in the Cradle pub closed for the day. Clifford Talbot was even more wrecked than usual because he had been waiting on the doorstep when the pub opened up and he was the last to leave. Bearing in mind that this was God's day, he was convinced that the Good Saviour would put in an appearance, but there had been no sign of him. Refusing to leave just in case God arrived late, he was quickly and forcefully ushered from the premises and the door was slammed and bolted behind him.

The last of the daylight had now faded and Gate Town's street lamps provided a weak orangey light through the fog as Talbot unsteadily made his way home. He had intended to go back to God's house in Princess Mary Road and keep vigil. But he decided it was too far to walk in his present state and he'd be better off going home and having a kip first. So, singing a mumbled version of 'Away in a Manger', he turned into what seemed an even murkier Chain Lane.

As he reached the dark and shuttered betting shop, Talbot stopped and had a piss. He then saw a lighted window in the flat above and shouted loudly up at it until the window was opened and Mrs. Pomfret looked out. Still shouting, Talbot announced that he'd be round after Christmas to collect his winnings because he now knew where God lived. He then proceeded to give rambling directions, followed by a suggestion that if she cared to accompany him right now he'd prove it by showing her. But before he had even finished saying what he had to say, Mrs. Pomfret had shut the window.

Yet Talbot didn't have to go that far to be reunited with his God. At this moment in time the 'Good Lord' also happened to be in Chain Lane.

Since being watched very carefully by some crank in the Cat in the Cradle pub, Shad was now making doubly sure he stayed away from the place, whatever the temptations. He was still enjoying his time here in the past. He was also proud of the way he had achieved it. Glad they had given him this journeyman assignment. And glad he had tricked them. He had visited the small, dull pub off the beaten track again. But once more it was inhabited by dull people. Not even the reasonably attractive, middle-aged slag of a barmaid was there. So he had come to Chain Lane in search of 'love'. But he was to be disappointed yet again. It was even worse than the previous evening. There wasn't one solitary whore out working this night. Not even a desperate one.

Therefore Shad was quietly angry. And when he was in that kind of mood he was at his murderous best and capable of killing just for the sake of it, without even the need of 'love'.

And then he saw them as they loomed out of the fog. It was a family, well wrapped up against the cold. It consisted of a father, a mother, a girl of about ten and a boy of no more than five or six. The girl held the boy's hand and the dad was holding a carrier bag with some wrapped gifts inside. They were obviously on their way home or going to visit someone. So Shad followed them. Not too close. Not yet. He would have preferred someone three or four years older but he decided that the young girl would have to do for now. His plan was to follow them and attack them at the right moment before they reached their destination. He would kill the parents and the small boy, then stun the girl before carrying her away to some secluded spot.

Despite the weather, it was a cheerful family. They laughed and joked as they walked on through the fog. The man had his free arm around his wife's shoulder. The young girl skipped and playfully teased her brother.

Shad put his hand in his pocket and activated the silks. He could feel them move, ready and waiting for his command.

Up ahead, the family had disappeared around a bend in the lane, but Shad could still hear them. He quickened his step. He then heard something else, a drunken voice wishing the family a happy Christmas and the man and woman and young girl returning the greeting. Shad swore to himself. The last thing he needed was a witness. And how many others were there? He then stopped as a figure appeared out of the fog.

It was the lunatic from the pub.

Once more, Talbot was lost in wonder as he saw Shad. He sank to his knees, put his hands together and began to pray at the top of his voice. 'We praise you, Father of all. We thank you for calling us to be your people, and for choosing us to give you glory…'

Shad had already taken his hand from his pocket and the foggy darkness was lit by a blaze of flashing electric colours as the silks flew from his hand. They flickered at great speed towards Talbot, slashing at his clothes and his skin before wrapping themselves swiftly around his throat.

Further along Chain Lane the young boy had turned to look. 'Fireworks,' he said.

His parents and sister also stopped and looked. The colourful lights from the silks could be seen through the darkness.

'Can't be fireworks,' said the father. 'They make a noise.'

'Just Christmas lights,' said the mother. 'Come on.' She shepherded them onwards as, back along the lane, Shad summoned the silks from Talbot's mutilated body and the lights faded.

16

The Walholme hotel in Sutherland Avenue seemed only to cater for the over sixties. That was because anyone younger would probably only want to stay there once. Once was enough. And that suited the oldies that preferred it quiet and without the noise and inconvenience that younger people might bring. Although strangely enough all the Walholme members of staff were in their late teens or twenties. This was because the elderly owner was a mean bastard who hired them young and paid them the minimum wage knowing that most people of that age needed the work. But not many of them lasted long anyway. The suffocating atmosphere and what seemed like the ever pervading smell of cooked cabbage and floor polish used to get to them eventually.

The Walholme was not that big. And it

seemed out of place. It was like a seaside hotel that had found itself transported to a nondescript town many, many miles from the sea. But every Christmas the Walholme was unusually busy. This was because it was 'turkey and tinsel time', when, for some unknown reason, a coach party or two of very senior citizens would travel down from the north of England and stay at the hotel. Bonner reckoned they only stayed there because it was cheap and, as far as they were concerned, was far enough down south to be like going abroad.

The young hotel workers would dread 'turkey and tinsel time' because many of the visitors, or 'prunes' as they called them, were rude or deaf or both. And they complained a lot. But, worst of all, there would be lousy music and most of the old buggers would dance.

A couple of empty coaches were parked in the hotel car park as Bonner's car arrived. Mrs. O'Day climbed from the car and headed for the hotel entrance. Bonner followed her. He then noticed a sign in the window.

'It's a private do,' he said.

'So what?' said Mrs. O'Day.

Inside the Walholme a sad looking forty-year old man with a Saddam Hussein moustache was sitting on a rostrum and playing an early-eighties synthesizer.

The medium sized dance floor had been opened up and elderly couples were dancing to melodies such as, 'Magic Moments', or something safely upbeat like 'Green Door'. None of them looked particularly merry and not one of them seemed to converse with their partner as they danced. They simply shuffled around the floor, en masse, while those even less agile sat at tables and watched. There were one or two couples who could obviously still manage the odd spin and twirl if they were given a chance, but in that relatively small space they were cramped and thwarted by the shuffling throng.

Mrs. O'Day and Bonner entered and were approached by a receptionist who looked as though he had not long left school. With him was a mischievous looking waitress who was gathering up empty glasses.

'Is Eric here?' asked Mrs. O'Day.

Bonner was puzzled. 'Eric?' he said, half to himself.

'No,' said the receptionist. 'His sister's not well.'

This wasn't exactly true. As well as being mean, Eric the owner was also a lazy shit and had left the chef to run things. But at this moment the chef was busy and in a panic. So the young guns were in charge.

'Yeah, well, he knows me. Can we get a drink?' said Mrs. O'Day.

The receptionist looked unsure.

'Go on, Malc', said the waitress, looking even more devilish and in need of some kind of diversion. 'It's Christmas.'

'That's right,' said Mrs. O'Day with a threatening smile. 'It's fucking Christmas.'

The waitress led Mrs. O'Day and Bonner to a table then went to fetch Mrs. O'Day a gin and tonic. Bonner had settled for a half of beer. He was still puzzled. 'How come you use the Walholme, of all places?' he asked.

'I don't use it,' said Mrs. O'Day. She looked around her at the guests. 'Have you seen this lot? Most of 'em look as if they've had a near-life experience.'

'But you just asked the young fella…'

'For fuck's sake, Sol,' Mrs. O'Day interrupted him. 'Do I look that old?'

The waitress brought the drinks and set them down. Mrs. O'Day reached for her glass and poured in some tonic. She saw that Bonner was still looking curiously at her. She raised her voice over the sound of the music.

'If you must know, my ex-husband was twenty-four years older than me. He liked to come here. The place suited him. But it didn't suit me. I came here with him on a couple of occasions until I told him he could fucking stuff it.'

She took a long, grateful pull of her drink as the music stopped and some of the dancers creaked back to their tables. Bonner was surprised. This was the first time he'd heard Mrs. O'Day mention anything about her marriage.

'When you say, ex?'

'I left the miserable sod years ago.'

'So where is he now?'

'He dropped down dead. Year before last. It was the only good thing he ever did for me.'

Following a couple of bum notes, the synthesizer playing restarted.

'Last night's visitor, he was here on behalf of the faceless ones. Our bosses.'

It came out of the blue once more as Bonner idly watched the dancers inch and bump their way around the floor. They reminded him of clapped-out dodgem cars on low power. He looked at Mrs. O'Day.

'This visitor, does he have a name?'

'No. The people at his level don't give names. Those in between do. But they're just the pen pushers. The appointment makers. His sort aren't good at planned appointments. They prefer to arrive at short notice.'

'And how much power do these people have?'

'Under these circumstances, all the power in the world.'

Bonner thought about this for a moment. 'So what did he want?'

'Oh, nothing more than an update,' Mrs. O'Day said lightly, which made Bonner suspect that there was more to it. 'He likes what we're doing. How we're handling things.'

'Good.'

Mrs. O'Day finished her drink. 'But then again, he was a slimy bastard. He hinted a lot. From what I could work out they're making plans for our downtimers.'

'Any idea what kind of plans?'

'No. But knowing them I imagine it'll be something special.'

She caught the attention of the waitress and mimed that she'd like another drink. At the same time the synthesizer player attempted to jolly things up by suddenly switching to the tune, 'Oh, Oh, Antonio'. It was obviously meant to amuse and possibly encourage a sing-along. But no-one looked amused and no-one sang along as the dancers continued to move around the floor at more or less the same speed.

'And do you know the odd thing about that smarm and charm bastard?' Mrs. O'Day continued. 'There were times when I felt he was disappointed. Oh, he was fascinated by the kid with the man-made eyes. He couldn't be told enough about that. And that worried me. But all in all I felt he expected more from our illegal visitors. Not robots and ray guns and men in silver suits, exactly. But something much more formidable. Because, when you think about it, Sol, these detainees are not exactly an impressive bunch are they? I mean, while we, the custodians of Gate Town, have been busily and vigilantly manning the watchtowers, there hasn't been much of an invasion from those of the future. Counting the child, we've only been invaded by three and a half downtimers, and one of those arrived dead.'

As the music continued, Mrs. O'Day decided to join in with the chorus.

'Oh, oh, Antonio,

He's gone away…'

A mummified looking couple at the next table stared at Mrs. O'Day as if she were committing a crime. It encouraged her to sing even louder.

'Left me alone-ee-oh,

All on my own-ee-oh…'

As Allie arrived at the gates of the laboratory she could hear the sirens of emergency vehicles moving through the foggy town. She was not happy about being summoned by Kenneth and had made up her mind that this had better be good. Or else.

He met her at the gate, and, as he led her through the cold building, smugly informed her that 'her special border force' was not doing a very good job with its crack down on illegal immigrants, because they seemed to have let one in. And one with a difference.

In the lab, he carefully took a couple of the threadlets from the specimen jar while Allie stood near him. She, too, shivered at the cold. And he could smell her perfume. To him, it wasn't sweet and sickly like a lot of young women's perfumes, or like the English lavender muck that his mother dabbed behind her ears. It was sharper and tangier, more like a man's expensive aftershave. He felt that it suited her, suited that faint air of masculinity that she had and which appealed to him.

As he set the threadlets on the plate of the manipulator he told her that they appeared to be made from some kind of synthetic silk which seemed to him to be totally indestructible. He said he had no idea where the source material was, but wished he had. Allie asked him where he had found them.

'On the body of the murdered schoolgirl,' he told her.

Kenneth was to be given even more of a treat as Allie grabbed him, eased him forcefully aside, and then took over proceedings. She peered through the lenses at the threadlets.

'It's as if they shouldn't be here,' he said, staying close to her. 'Shouldn't exist. They're like something that hasn't been invented yet. And they can move. These little bits of shit can really move. By themselves. I mean, if something so small can be that strong, imagine what the source material must be like. And that material has got to be around somewhere. It must still be with the girl's killer.'

Allie continued to study the fibres. 'How much does your group know about this?'

'I haven't had chance to tell them yet.'

'What about the Major Crime Squad?'

'The same.'

'Good. Keep it that way.'

'Eh?'

Allie looked up from the apparatus. 'It means you *don't* tell them. And you don't let any of this stuff out of your sight. Do you understand?'

'No. I don't understand…'

Allie raised her voice. 'Just fucking listen to me,

Ken.'

'Sorry.'

'I'll spell it out to you. You tell no-one about this until you're asked. *Now* do you understand?'

Kenneth nodded. Allie smelling so wonderful, and being strong with him and giving him orders, he found that pleasurable. He would do anything for that.

'And don't let anyone else in here unless I tell you.'

Kenneth nodded obediently once more as Allie took her mobile from her pocket.

Whilst taking Mrs. O'Day home along Chain Lane, Bonner was forced to stop his car by a barrier of police and other emergency vehicles, along with flashing lights, noisy radios and hi-viz jackets moving busily through the fog.

Bonner climbed from the car, showed his warrant card and pushed his way past uniformed police officers and medics to the centre of the operation. Lit by crime scene lights, Talbot's body was lying spread-eagled on the pavement. Bonner took a closer look. The lacerated clothing and flesh and marks to the neck reminded him of another victim he had once seen, the dead girl by the Connaught cemetery. It was at that moment that his phone rang.

'Yes?' He moved away from the noise and bustle so that he could hear the message more clearly.

'Sir,' said Allie on the phone. 'The downtimers. It's possible that we haven't got them all. There could still be one around.'

Bonner was stunned. He turned to find Mrs. O'Day beside him, watching him, seeing the look on his face.

After Shad had left the B&B, Sylvia had waited for his return by listening out and by occasionally peeping from the front window. If indeed he had needed a walk she hadn't expected it to take very long. But after about an hour and a half had passed she assumed that he had found some form of entertainment somewhere and would possibly be out for a while longer. So she had decided to take another look inside his room. 'Come on,' she said to Raymond as she led the way into the hallway.

But Raymond wasn't sure about this. As he had already told Sylvia, their guest had paid for his room and had caused no trouble.

Fidgety and impatient, Sylvia turned on him. 'I said, come on. I want to show you what I saw.'

She took the master key from her cardigan

pocket as she climbed the stairs. Raymond hesitated for a moment longer before following her up on to the landing and to the door of Shad's room. Sylvia unlocked the door and opened it. The room was as neat and tidy as ever.

'There,' she said. 'It was in there.' She indicated the lowest drawer in the chest of drawers.

'What was?'

'A light. A coloured light. A kind of glow.'

She knelt down to open the drawer. It still held papers and envelopes, the recent copies of the Gate Town Gazette and the street map. This time Sylvia had a thorough search through the items. Wondering how they would explain themselves, Raymond peered nervously out of the open doorway in the hope that their guest wouldn't suddenly return.

Sylvia had found one used A4 envelope that was quite bulky. She peeked inside it. She then gave a little gasp of surprise. 'Money,' she said. 'All this money.' She showed the opened envelope to Raymond. It was packed with paper currency.

'For God's sake put it back,' said Raymond.

'But why does he have so much money?'

'I don't know. But it's his.'

'Perhaps he's a criminal.'

'Oh, don't be so stupid.' For once Raymond

was answering back. 'It's probably his savings. Money he lives on. So where's this light you were talking about?'

Sylvia gave him a baleful look before replacing the envelope of money and continuing with her search. Then the glow appeared. It shimmered faintly at first. And it was inside what looked like a slim, plastic folder at the bottom of the drawer.

'You see?' said Sylvia, triumphantly.

She lifted the folder from the drawer and found that the shimmering light was emanating from a strange piece of membrane-like material inside the folder.

'Sylvia, please!' protested Raymond. 'Leave it alone. It's probably something to do with his stage act.'

Sylvia was furious with Raymond for daring to call her stupid. It was something she was determined to make him pay for later. In the meantime, she remained defiant.

'Well, let's see what it does, then, shall we?' she said as she withdrew the mysterious piece of lightweight material, which was roughly the size of a large postcard, halfway out from the folder.

Like the pencil case moment in Eve's makeshift cell, the B&B room was suddenly filled with brightly moving images. But this time it was on a far larger and longer scale. Figures and colours radiated and swirled around the room, projecting themselves on to the walls, the mirror, the wardrobe, the window frame, and the open door, then around and around and again and again.

Sylvia and Raymond stared in astonishment as a garish and slightly grainy old film began to take shape. There were the motor coaches parked up and waiting in Dunstall & Sons' yard on that sunny August morning so long ago. There were the members of staff. There was Mr. Edward, Mr. Michael and Mr. Stanley. There was Karen and her young son. And the happy figures looked out from Ferry Lane of old. They waved. They smiled into camera. They mouthed silent words as around and around the room they flickered and span, as if for ever.

Sylvia and Raymond were so transfixed by what they were seeing that they failed to hear the front door opening and closing, and the sound of Shad climbing the stair.

Raymond was the first to die. He had stepped out from the room to be met by yet another light show. This time it was the silks twisting and turning in the air as they left Shad's hand. There was a window on the landing that looked out over the back yard. The silks lifted Raymond as if he were a small child and flung him with great force into the window, smashing glass panes and wooden frame in the process and pitching him headfirst down on to the concrete yard below.

Sylvia emerged from the room and screamed. Shad then redirected the silks and they followed the terrified woman as she ran down the stairs and tried to hide. With a signal-like movement of his hand, Shad had manage to slow down the silks so that they deliberately took their time in finding Sylvia, thereby prolonging her terror. She had slammed the lounge door on them but they flattened themselves and wriggled underneath, then followed her into the kitchen. Still screaming, she fled into the small utility room and tried to unlock the rear door. But the silks had reached her before she could open it. Unlike Talbot and Raymond, Shad made sure that Sylvia's death was noisy and lengthy. He watched with satisfaction as the silks ripped at her and tore every last shred of clothing from her body before they coiled themselves around her throat and slowly strangled her.

17

Despite it being Christmas evening, Charnham Cross had suddenly sprung into life. Necessary staff members had been called back from the holiday to join the few that had remained on duty. Mrs. O'Day was drinking copious amounts of strong coffee as she got things up and running. With the possibility of them being in for a long session, overnight accommodation at the camp had been organised for her and for Bonner, Pierce and Allie.

Whilst quietly recovering from the Choudhury shindig, Pierce had been summoned. He and a hastily put-together team had taken over the crime scene in Chain Lane, creating an even larger no-go area and keeping all evidence and information for themselves. Although Talbot had yet to be identified, his remains had already been shipped to the mortuary at Charnham Cross.

A second team had descended upon the laboratory, and, under instructions from Allie, had taken away all of Fuckhead Ken's evidence and notes along with his specimens and equipment, leaving him with nothing.

Standing by the gate to watch the vehicles drive away, Kenneth felt sad that Allie had not thanked him or bothered to say goodbye. But at least he had been close to her and her perfume for a while and he was grateful for that. He was also looking forward to thinking about her fairly vigorously that night in his lonely bed.

At Charnham Cross, Allie had explained to Mrs. O'Day and Bonner that it was possible for a present day killer to have access to the strange fibre, but she believed that that was unlikely. She was therefore convinced that the material was alien and not of this time.

She then took them to her lab and showed them Kenneth's findings including a demonstration of the mysterious threads of fibre. 'We could be dealing with a downtimer who's using material brought from the future,' she announced. 'One who likes to kill.'

Mrs. O'Day swore under her breath as she took another look at the threadlets.

'Could there be more than one killer?' asked

Bonner.

'Can't be sure,' said Allie. 'Might know more when we've done further tests.'

Bonner turned to Mrs. O'Day. He spoke quietly. 'Your fella with no name is gonna love this.'

As they walked from the lab, Mrs. O'Day gave orders to Bonner. 'Get the local police out. Let's fuck up their Christmas as well. Tell them there's no description as yet, but we're looking for a lunatic. That's all they need to know.'

Bonner went to the mortuary at nine-fifteen that evening and used his mobile to take a head and shoulders photo of Talbot. He then rang home to explain his overnight stay at the camp. But Lesley had obviously gone to bed because there was no reply. So he left a message. This put him in a bad mood because he would like to have had a sensible conversation with his wife, but such an option seemed out of the question these days. And the last thing he needed right now was to be on the wrong side of her when he had to find an excuse to see Jace tomorrow, as promised.

On his way across the old parade ground Bonner thought about another excuse he may have to work on one day in the future. A big bloody excuse. And a hurtful one. A reason to leave his wife and set up home with Jace, if that was at all possible. Although right now it didn't bear thinking about for too long.

Bonner didn't really do love. Not big time love. Not those overblown declarations of love. Not all that 'till the seas run dry, twelfth of never' crap. He had always cared deeply for Lesley. But now, as she slowly but surely distanced herself from him, he found that he needed Jace much more, and would hate never to be with her again.

Thinking back, he remembered a time long ago when he might well have known love without fully realising it. He was twenty-one and he was going out with a girl of sixteen, who, unlike Jace, looked and acted older than her years. She had insisted on taking him for a drink one summer lunchtime because she wanted to have a serious talk with him. She had also insisted that the drinks were on her.

Bonner remembered that the sun shone brightly that day. And the pub was called 'The Sun'. And the girl was blonde. Golden blonde. Of course, the weed that Bonner was smoking at the time had enhanced all the golds and the yellows, including the brass ornaments in the bar, the amber curtains, the Wills's Gold Flake ashtrays, and the lemons that the barman was slicing up behind the bar. The spliff had also made him laugh out loud to himself when he thought that all it needed right now was to find custard coloured sick in the loo, or to have Donovan singing 'Yellow fucking Mellow' on the juke box.

It was then that the girl had told him, in her worldly-wise and grown-up way, that she was dumping him for good. And his stupid, dope influenced laugh probably hadn't helped his cause.

Bonner had never forgotten that girl. Or the moment. And, as he reached the blockhouse, he realised that that might well have been love. He also realised that Jace came as close to that girl as anyone else ever had.

As he entered the protective storage unit he found Pierce watching as the property officer bagged and labelled the victim's few pathetic possessions.

'We've got a name and address for him at last,' Pierce told Bonner as he picked up a grubby Benefits Agency letter. 'Found it on this.' He read aloud, 'Clifford George Talbot.' He handed the item to the property officer. 'One less payment for us poor taxpayers to worry about.'

Bonner had reacted to the name. He tried to recall where he'd heard it. 'Clifford?' he asked himself aloud. He then remembered the conversation with

Mrs. Pomfret in her betting shop.

'And there's this,' said Pierce as he produced Talbot's now crumpled postcard.

Bonner took the cheap card. He looked at the flashy and colourful figure of Christ raising the dead. 'Of course. Cliff Talbot.'

'You know him?' asked Pierce.

'No. But I've heard all about him. He's the man who met God.'

At the B&B in Princess Mary Road, 'God' was enjoying himself.

Shad had intended to get away from the house as soon as possible after killing his hosts, but, on attempting to start their Renault Clio, found that he had no idea how to operate a small but complicated vehicle that relied upon liquid fuel and was not guided by a remote command system. Convinced that no-one would come looking just yet, not in this desert of a place, he decided to rest up in the house until the next day, mainly because those old body repairs of his, or 'join-up-jobs' as journeymen liked to call them, were giving him a fair amount of distress.

In the meantime he had taken down both the B&B vacancy sign and the Christmas tree to avoid attracting attention. With plenty of Christmas food at hand, plus some good wine and brandy, he had prepared himself a fine feast on Raymond and Sylvia's best dining table, whilst playing their easy-listening CD's on the music system.

Earlier, he had dragged the battered body of Raymond in from the yard and laid it out on the floor of the utility room. He had then pulled down the dead man's trousers and underpants before arranging Sylvia's naked body on top of it in the sixty-nine position. Shad had enjoyed his humiliation of the dead. His guess was that Sylvia had probably always been strictly missionary, and even then it would have been under sufferance. So it amused him to think that only in death could she be seen taking part in a sixty-niner.

Len Chalk, fifty-eight year old landlord of Talbot's bedsit in Chapel Street, had no objection to Bonner and Pierce calling on him at ten past ten on Christmas evening. He lived alone and he liked to talk, but his two other tenants were sleeping off the topped-up, all-hours-joined-into-one sleep of the true alchy. And his telly had broken down, so there was fuck all else to do. As he led the way up the stairs he said he was sorry to be told about Mr. Talbot's demise, although it would mean extra work sorting out the room. He explained that he

PJ Hammond

was a good landlord because in taking most of his tenants' benefit money he was helping them to spend less on booze.

'Did he have any friends?' asked Pierce.

'Not that I can think of.'

'Family?'

'No. He never mentioned family.'

'What about God?' asked Bonner.

'Eh?' said the landlord as they reached the door of Talbot's room.

'Did he talk about God?'

'Well, yes, he had been banging on about God a bit just lately. I expect that's because it's Christmas.'

Bonner and Pierce reacted to the smell of the room as they entered. They looked around them at the sad, shithouse state of Talbot's last place of refuge.

'Where did he drink?' asked Pierce.

'The Cat in the Cradle. He only ever went there.'

Pierce opened the door of the wardrobe. The stench of months of piss soaked clothes and shoes and wood was overpowering.

'Would you like a cup of tea while you're here?' asked Len Chalk.

'No, thanks,' said Bonner.

There was no welcome whatsoever for Bonner and Pierce when they knocked loudly on the door of the Cat in the Cradle pub just after eleven p.m.

The landlord and landlady, Rick and Debs, were in their late thirties. Because of the beer, Rick had gone to seed early, while Debs made a habit of wearing the wrong clothes because she liked to think she looked younger, which she didn't. They were proud of the fact that in three years they had turned what they saw as a quiet pub for dull people into a fun place. And fun for Rick and Debs meant loud music, loud people and a steep rise in the price of a pint.

As Rick turned on a couple of bar lights, Debs complained about being disturbed when they were enjoying a much needed bit of time to themselves. She was obviously a born complainer and continued to bellyache until Bonner took out his phone and showed her the photo of Talbot. That shut her up. She sat her plump arse down on a chair and looked as though she was about to be sick.

'Do you recognise him?'

Debs nodded. Her husband took a look at the picture. 'Bloody hell! What happened?'

'He met with an accident,' said Bonner.

'But he was only in here lunchtime.' said Debs. 'He was the last to leave.'

245

'What time was this?'

'About half past four.'

'Was he with anyone?' asked Pierce.

Rick shook his head. 'No. He was always on his own. Just a pisshead. Not the kind we want here. But he never caused trouble.' He took another look at the photo. 'Poor sod.'

Bonner closed the picture. He put the phone back in his pocket. 'Was he in here last night?'

'Don't know. We had the night off. Took some presents over to Debs' mum and dad.'

'When he was in here lunchtime, did you talk to him?'

'No-one used to talk to him if they could help it.'

'He did all the talking,' added Debs. 'Mostly to himself. 'Always going on about God.' She got up from the chair. 'Who wants to listen to that?' She started to do a bit of unnecessary tidying. Like most good moaners she was a compulsive tidier.

Rick grinned. 'He even reckoned he *saw* God once. In here, of all places. Over there.'

He pointed to the rostrum. Bonner and Pierce turned to look. The structure looked tacky and sad in the semi-darkness.

'It was just some fella. Some sort of entertainer.'

'Employed by you?' asked Pierce

'No. Just part of the crowd. We was busy that night and he just got up and did this trick.'

'What sort of trick?'

'Kelly, one of our barmaids. He lifted her up. On a chair.'

'What's so marvellous about that?' said Bonner.

'He didn't even touch her. Or the chair.'

Bonner made his way to the rostrum. The others followed him.

'Had you seen this man before?' asked Pierce.

'No,' said Rick.

'Or since?'

Rick shook his head.

'So you wouldn't know his name?'

'No.'

'So what did he look like?' asked Bonner.

Debs had gathered up a couple of beer mats that were hiding under a table. 'Tall. Thin. But strong looking. Long face.'

Bonner picked up a chair. He carried it up on to the rostrum. He sat down on it. 'So how did he do his trick?'

'Dunno.' said Rick. 'It was all sort of quick.'

'Very quick,' said Debs.

'And it was busy in here, remember?' Rick added. 'People moving to and fro. But he seemed to take something from his pocket.'

'Like what?'

'Well, it sort of looked like a bunch of ribbons. All strung together. And he whirled them around the chair. And they lit up. Like Christmas lights. And the bloody chair just lifted. Straight up in the air. On its own.'

Debs had stopped fussing around. 'Not ribbons,' she said, remembering. 'More like silks. My gran, she used to do embroidery. Used to buy these silks. All sorts of bright colours. They looked a bit like them. Only what he used seemed to be electric. The way they lit up.'

Bonner looked at Pierce. He got up from the chair. He stepped down from the rostrum.

18

Mrs. O'Day and her team were up extra early at Charnham Cross on Boxing Day morning. Eve was woken by nurse Claire at six-thirty a.m. and told to be prepared for an interview. And the busy sounds of people moving to and fro along the iron gantry roused David Doughty from his sleep.

By eight a.m. the overnight fog had gone. But the sky was overcast and the day was cold. Claire led a warmly wrapped up Cara across the compound to the activity centre while the child's mother sat waiting in the interview room.

Mrs. O'Day had managed to get a short but much needed amount of sleep, and she now looked businesslike as she entered the interview room. Bonner and Pierce were with her. They pulled up chairs and sat at the table while the guard left, locking the door behind her. But Mrs. O'Day was in no mood to sit down. She kept her eyes on Eve as Bonner started both the camera recorder and the audio interview recorder.

'Now let's familiarise ourselves, shall we?' Mrs. O'Day began. 'You've told us your name is Eve Palmer. Although there's no way of us proving that. Not that it really matters. You've arrived from over a hundred years in the future, bringing your four year old daughter with you. But you can't tell us how you got here, because you were asleep at the time. And it doesn't work unless you're asleep. Right, so far?'

'Yes.'

'I spoke with your daughter, Mrs. Palmer. 'She told me she remembers coming here. She saw images.'

Eve did not reply.

'So how could that have happened? Did she cheat? Did she open those pretty little artificial eyes of hers and take a peek? Or maybe she was dreaming.'

Once more, Eve did not reply.

'Somehow I don't think so. I think she's telling the truth. Because she's a child and no-one could expect her to tell lies in order not to give the game away. Unlike you and Mr. Doughty. Am I right?'

Eve considered this for a moment. It was true that part of her Timelight briefing was not to reveal the actual mechanics of travelling back. She had remembered seeing an image, then an extremely bright blue light that had made her close her eyes. Then it was over and she was here, back in the past. She now considered that admitting to that small part of the process was not too much of an indiscretion. So she nodded in reply to the question.

'Thank you, said Mrs. O'Day. 'Now at the time of being taken into custody you told my officers that you and others like you brought nothing with you from the future that could be unfairly used to your advantage, because that was not permitted.'

'That's right,' said Eve.

'Well, isn't that thoughtful of the people who sent you here? How good of them to make sure that none of you could go out of your way to fuck up the past.'

'I have already explained this,' said Eve.

'Then explain something else,' said Mrs. O'Day. 'Because there are things we can't work out. Things that are too far ahead of us.' She looked at Pierce. 'Tell her'

'A transparent gel,' Pierce said to Eve. 'One that can be poured over someone's face and cures a common cold in a matter of seconds. If it can do that it must be able to cure a lot of other complaints. And we don't have anything like that. We wish we had. It could help so many people. It could also make someone a fortune. I know it defeats the purpose, but there are also those who would kill for such a product.'

Eve was surprised and disturbed by what had been said. 'That can't be. You've got it wrong. Something must be wrong.'

'Oh, you bet it is,' said Mrs. O'Day. 'So what is this wonder cure?'

'There is such a healing balm. It cures most ailments although it can't cure serious illnesses or injuries. But you must be mistaken. Even though it could help us, none of us would be allowed to bring that medication back. As you've said, if it got into the wrong hands…'

'Which it obviously has,' said Pierce. 'Because it's here. It's been used.'

Eve reached for a bottle of water. 'The man who's detained here. Did he have it?'

'No.'

Eve fumbled with the cap of the bottle. Pierce helped her with the bottle. He poured a cup of water for her.

'All right, then,' said Eve, 'the body you showed me, the man who arrived dead. He must have brought some with him.'

Pierce shook his head.

'Well I certainly didn't bring it.'

'We know that.'

Eve tried to think back. Who, in her time, would be stupid enough to do this? To make such a mistake. Or allow it to happen. She could think of no-one.

'And there's worse to come,' said Mrs. O'Day. She looked at Bonner as she lit a cigarette.

Bonner leant forward in his chair. 'Something that looks like a bunch of ribbons and lights strung together. Made from a material that would seem to be unknown to us. Something that has incredible strength considering its structure. Yet something that can be operated. Something that can be used to kill.'

Eve held the cup of water tightly with both hands. She then realised that her hands were trembling.

'Could you tell us what that item might be?' asked Bonner.

Eve said nothing.

'We have to know. Now. It's vitally important.'

Again Eve said nothing. She closed her eyes, hoping it would help her to control her shaking.

Mrs. O'Day's voice rang out. 'Listen to what's being said, will you?' She moved to the table. She sat down at last. She dragged her chair in close to Eve. 'It seems that someone from the future, from your time in the future, has come here and has killed. Not just once. But twice.'

With eyes still closed, Eve shuddered violently. She crushed the paper cup in her hands. Water splashed over her. She opened her eyes. Involuntarily, she dabbed needlessly at the water that had soaked her clothes.

'Leave it!' Mrs. O'Day ordered.

Eve stopped what she was doing. She continued to tremble.

'We need to find this person or persons as quickly as possible. Do you understand that?'

Eve nodded. She clasped her hands together.

'You said you were hoping that someone would come back to help you.'

Eve nodded.

'Are we talking about a colleague?'

'Possibly.'

'And could one of your colleagues be capable of killing?'

'No. Why would they? It's against everything they stand for. Everything we've been taught. Except...' She stopped.

'Except what?' said Mrs. O'Day.

Eve was wondering if she was saying too much. And was this another trap. She decided not to answer.

Mrs. O'Day watched her for a moment. She then deliberately softened her tone just a fraction. 'You said you don't want your daughter to spend the rest of her life in a prison.'

Eve spoke in almost a whisper. 'That's right.'

'Well, if you help us, maybe I can do something.'

Bonner was surprised at this. He glanced at Pierce. Pierce gave a 'Don't ask me' shrug.

'But on one condition,' Mrs. O'Day continued. 'And that is that we get no more bullshit from you. We get the truth. Not just some of it. All of it. How you got here. Everything.' She paused for a moment. 'Otherwise there's no deal.

She shoved back her chair. She got up from the table. She turned away. She lit a fresh cigarette from the one she had half smoked.

Eve looked down at her damp, clasped hands. She had gripped them so tightly that the knuckles hurt. She asked herself if it really mattered if this was a trap, because these people already seemed to know so much. And she knew she had to help them. Not just for her daughter's sake, but because of whoever it was that had been sent back to kill and to cause havoc.

'All right,' she said, at last, 'Timelight may have sent journeymen to look for Cara and me.'

Mrs. O'Day turned back to the table. 'Sent

what?'

'The dead man. I recognised the scar tissue on his body. The amount of work that had obviously been done, and the procedure. He would have to have been a journeyman.'

'So what do these journeymen do?'

'They… they specialize in finding people, usually in difficult and dangerous situations.'

Mrs. O'Day sat back down at the table. 'And the ribbons with lights?'

'They're called silks.'

'The landlady of the pub said they looked like silks,' said Bonner.

'So what are they used for?' Mrs. O'Day asked.

'They were first created as a kind of novelty. Then, because of their power, they were used in engineering. And in security. Then their manufacture was discontinued.'

'Why?'

'Because they were made in such a way that they could produce their own power.'

'How?'

'By growing it.'

'By what?'

'We have machines that can design, make and repair themselves. They've been taught to do that. But the silks were found to malfunction if they managed to cause damage to other power sources, particularly those they were incompatible with. Therefore they were seen as a threat and were banned.'

Mrs. O'Day thought about this for a moment. 'These journeymen of yours. Would they have used the healing balm?'

'Yes. In normal circumstances in our time it would be part of their equipment. Their operations are mostly hazardous. And a lot of them are in a constant state of reassembly.'

'What does that mean?'

'It means their bodies have been broken and mended too many times.

'And the silks? Would journeymen use those?'

Eve hesitated.

'Well?'

'Probably, yes, before they were banned.'

'What about after they were banned?'

'Only those journeymen who couldn't be trusted.'

'And do you trust these people?'

'They could sometimes be unpredictable. It was in their nature. All part of the damage that's been done to them.'

'And could that make these journeymen dangerous?'

'It's possible. But they would only be employed as a last resort. And, as a precaution, each set of silks would be shared.'

'Shared?'

Eve hesitated once more. 'Yes. Journeymen always work in pairs.'

On hearing this, Mrs. O'Day looked at Bonner and Pierce, then back.

'Oh, great! An unsafe product and unsafe people let loose. Sent back to kill.'

'Please,' said Eve, 'listen to me. None of us would have expected this. And if I'd known this would happen I would never have come here. I would never have volunteered.'

'So what the hell were you and your colleagues playing at?' Mrs. O'Day replied. 'You arrive here with fake currency and fake documents that are so good that they can go undetected. And the very fact that you and your bits and pieces can travel back in time in the first place is a marvel in itself. And yet, for all its ingenuity and resources, this Timelight outfit of yours got things wrong. They've more or less abandoned you and your child. Why?'

Having no other option now but to tell all, Eve began to relax. Her hands stopped shaking. It was like something she'd once read about condemned people, facing death or a life sentence, suddenly finding an inner calm and resignation. Because she was well aware that there was no hope for her now. No-one was coming to help. All she could rely on was that this woman would keep her word and try to make sure her daughter had some kind of a life.

She spoke quietly as she told her questioners that Timelight was a highly secret experiment, known to only a chosen few members of those in authority. She then explained that as an historian she had been asked to work on the project. This meant living on site and having no contact with the outside world until the work was completed. Cara was allowed to be with her.

'And allowed to travel back with you?' asked Mrs. O'Day.

'Yes. That was part of the experiment.'

'To take such a risk with a small, vulnerable child?'

'She was in my care.'

'That doesn't exactly fill me with confidence,' said Mrs. O'Day.

When asked how many people worked on the project, Eve told them that the number was between thirty and forty but she only knew a few of them personally. There were other departments. And they were kept in separate units. The Timelight project had been worked on for many years, with some reversals, before achieving success. Yet it was still an ongoing experiment using a programme that could go back to a specific moment in time. Back to some random, life-changing event. Nothing big. Just something simple. Something ordinary. But an event all the same. This was to ensure, at that stage, that nothing of historical importance could be accidentally changed, leading to calamitous results. Eve then went on to explain that even after all the years of hard work and careful planning it had not exactly been easy to get here.

'Fine,' said Mrs. O'Day, 'but you still haven't told us what went wrong?'

Yet again, Eve hesitated. 'I believe- well, I was aware that some last minute decisions may have been made.'

'What kind of decisions?'

'The departure procedure, it may have been brought forward in a hurry.'

'You mean it was rushed?'

'Well- yes,' said Eve.

'Why?'

'Well, it was- it was discovered that there was a possibility of competition. A scientist who had once worked for us had defected.'

'Taking all his knowledge with him?'

'Yes.'

'Where? To some other outfit?'

'I'm afraid so, yes.'

Mrs. O'Day leant back in her chair. She sighed. She looked at Bonner. 'What was I saying about getting some bad shit?'

'Big achievements,' said Pierce. 'First to climb Everest. First men on the moon. Everyone wants to get there first. Everyone wants a rosette and a medal. And travelling back in time? That has to be the biggest one of all. They couldn't pass up on that, could they?'

Mrs. O'Day wasn't so sure. She turned back to Eve. 'So you and your kid and the others were bundled all the way here in a bit of a panic.'

'It wasn't exactly a panic.'

'You told us you couldn't do the return trip without help.'

'That's right.'

'Have you tried?'

'Yes, on two occasions. When things had got desperate.'

'So what happened?'

'The Timelight failed to capture. It depends upon the donors, you see.'

'Donors?' asked Bonner.

'Yes,' said Eve, 'because what we've achieved isn't magic. And it isn't luck. It's nothing more than science.' She looked at Mrs. O'Day. 'You asked me once if we'd proved the existence of God. Well, we haven't. And we probably never will. But we did find something. We found a way of using the souls of the dead. Even those who are long dead.'

Mrs. O'Day and Bonner and Pierce stared at her in disbelief. In response, Eve gave just the tiniest smile of self-satisfaction.

'They are the donors,' she said.

19

Sunny August the fifth, nineteen-sixty-one, in all its happy, vivid, Kodak Brownie splendour, had been set loose in the large empty space of the disused hospital ward in present day Charnham Cross. As the Timelight shapes and figures swirled smoke-like around the room, the line-up of cheerful day-trippers spoke silent words and gave their final farewell waves. Mr. Michael was smiling, whilst his elder brothers beamed with company pride.

The doors of the ward had been locked and a small audience sat on four dilapidated chairs and stared as the sunlit images of their very own Ferry Lane from long ago, swung and twisted around and around them. The spellbound audience members were Mrs. O'Day, Bonner, Pierce and Allie.

Following the interview, Eve had led Mrs. O'Day

and Bonner to the side ward and surrendered up the pencil case. 'Something you missed,' she had told them. She had unzipped the case, and, from between the sleeve of false lining had withdrawn a section of the shimmering Timelight membrane, similar to the one that Sylvia had found to her cost in Shad's room. She had handled the material carefully, explaining that whilst it was fairly strong, it was not as indestructible as the silks. She had then revealed that although communication with her colleagues had broken down, the Timelight remained active as it was forever searching for any donor, or soul, because, having nowhere else to go, many of the souls waited even long after the host body had decayed. Then, when a soul is eventually found and locked onto, it is called a capture and certain people can be sent back providing they are suitable candidates.

'What do you mean by suitable?' Mrs. O'Day had asked.

'Close enough to the images,' was Eve's reply. 'A reasonable match.'

'Like a woman and child, for instance?'

'Yes.'

In the disused hospital ward, the shifting images now showed the Dunstall & Sons' employees preparing to board the coaches. Young mum Karen blew a goodbye kiss at the camera and her son waved happily.

'A picture, a light, and a small ghost,' said Mrs. O'Day.

Bonner had a wry smile to himself. He'd come close by suggesting it might be something to do with photography, but he doubted if Mrs. O'Day would ever give him credit for that.

The shapes and colours of days gone by danced across Mrs. O'Day as she got up from her chair and moved to a small table in the centre of the ward. The pencil case and the piece of membrane lay on the table top. Mrs. O'Day eased the membrane back into its fake sleeve and the shapes and colours and sunshine and smiles and silent laughter were extinguished, like a film that had suddenly been switched off.

Pierce and Allie visited the protective storage unit and painstakingly searched through the effects of David Doughty. But no Timelight membrane was found. Neither was there one hidden amongst the clothing and the small amount of personal items belonging to the dead downtimer. As Eve and Cara had only needed one Timelight device between them, Pierce's guess was that if indeed two journeymen had been employed then one device would also have sufficed.

David Doughty's Boxing Day lunch was rudely interrupted by Bonner, Pierce and a couple of guards arriving without warning to turn over his living space before leaving him to be strip-searched by the military paramedics.

When Doughty was eventually bundled into the interview room to learn what the team now knew, he realised, like Eve, that there was little point in continuing to hide the truth. He admitted that he too was a volunteer, but from a different Timelight department to Eve. His work as a biotechnologist had earned him a place, although he had used his privilege of a trip back in time not to study and make reports, but to escape from a world that he no longer respected. And meeting Annette had reinforced his intention of not returning. So he had got rid of his Timelight membrane by burning it.

With nothing left to live for and with his patience exhausted, David Doughty turned on his captors at long last. In one fairly long rant he spoke of all the scientific advances that had been achieved in his time period, but to his mind had failed. He told them that because of the overuse of synthetic biology programmes and hybrid agriculture on a grand scale there was a serious and irreplaceable species decline. He complained that nothing was left to chance any more. And there were few surprises. To him it had become an unimaginative place, devoid of interest, where genetic engineering and regenerative medicine had tampered with all living things to such an extent that randomness was lost and only control for the sake of control remained.

'It's a fake world,' he said, with anger and despair. 'A manufactured world. So think yourselves lucky that you can still look at an unpolluted sky, can smell real flowers and real grass, and can look up into the branches and leaves of a real tree.'

But Bonner and Pierce were unimpressed. Outside the interview room they watched as Doughty was escorted back to his confinement quarters.

'Him and his fucking trees!' said Bonner.

Journeyman Shad woke up in the comfort of Raymond and Sylvia's flouncy double bed to find that it was mid-day. He was experiencing a good old-fashioned twenty-first century hangover. And those damaged nerves beneath his skin patches were causing him even more suffering. Having made up his mind that it would be wiser to make his getaway during darkness, he took a hot bath in the couple's pink walled bathroom.

As he lay in the soothing warmth of the water, Shad recalled when he and Joseph Valentine had first downtimed from the future to the Connaught cemetery. It was at dead of night. They had only got as far as the nearby lane before his companion had collapsed with serious breathing difficulties. Shad had made no attempt to save him, but had simply taken stock of his surroundings while waiting for the man to die. His unfortunate colleague was a stickler for protocol and considered himself to be a candidate for promotion. He was also prepared to attempt the bring-back task that had been assigned to them whilst taking every care not to damage the fabric of time and the people of the past. His assignment had been to locate a solitary male downtimer, while Shad's mission was to try to make contact with a woman and a small child who had also downtimed.

But Shad had made other plans for himself well before the pair of them were Timelighted back. So had Journeyman Joe not died he would have killed him at some point anyway. And now he would leave Gate Town for good and broaden his horizons by using his knowledge of the future to acquire both wealth and power.

Preparing himself for his evening departure, Shad had helped himself to Raymond and Sylvia's loose cash and credit cards, and had even managed to open up what he laughably regarded as their piece of primitive computing apparatus in order to try to access their bank accounts. But he was unsuccessful. In the process he had accidentally knocked over and smashed the bulb of a lighted desk lamp, causing some strands of the silks, which he always kept with him, to detached themselves from the bunch and viciously slashed at his arm before he managed to control them.

The inscription on the small headstone read, *'Noel Timothy Thomas - born April 4th 1956 – Died August 8th 1961 – Went away to be with Jesus.'*

Bonner was back in the Connaught cemetery once more. It was gone four p.m. and what there was of the daylight was beginning to fade. As he moved slowly past the accompanying headstones of Karen Anne Thomas, Anthony John Merrow and Frank Johnson, he took his mobile from his pocket and called his home number. He apologised to Lesley for being away all night, explaining that things were busy. He then tried calling Jace, but her line was engaged. He put the phone back in his pocket as the long tall figure of Pierce appeared out of the gathering dusk.

Jace, the other love of Bonner's life, was saddened. Christmas was almost over and she and Bonner had spent no real time together as he had promised. And their presents to each other remained under the tree, still unopened. Because she was upset she also realised that she didn't love Bonner just a bit, as she had told him, but probably a lot more. When he had tried to get through to her she had been answering a call from her colleague, Fran.

Even though it was Christmas, there was some work going. An out-of-towner businessman that Fran knew was on an emergency assignment and staying in a Gate Town hotel over the holiday period. Fran explained that he was a generous punter but he liked to do it with two girls, and was she willing? Jace had thought about this. For the time being she was still a working girl, therefore there was no point in turning down good money. And Bonner didn't look like appearing today. So she agreed.

Pierce had gathered all the necessary information about the nineteen-sixty-one coach crash. As he stood by the graves he scanned through his tablet and gave Bonner a run-down of the events of that sad day including the fact that poor young Noel had hung on for another three days before dying of his injuries.

Bonner looked around him in the growing darkness. 'Bloody lost souls, of all things.' He shivered and pulled up his collar. 'What next for fuck's sake?'

'You heard what the lady said. It's just science.'

'Fucking science!' said Bonner. He moved to examine the headstones of the neighbouring graves.

'Think about it,' said Pierce. 'We all know that people from a couple of hundred years ago could never have conceived that there would be such things as photographs, let alone moving films. First photos, eighteen-twenty-six. First movies, eighteen-eighty. And look what's been achieved since then.' He scanned through his tablet once more. 'I mean, have you ever watched those jerky old black and white street scenes and wondered where the various people were going to or coming from? Or what they had in their pockets? Or what their home life was like?'

'No,' said Bonner as he studied the headstones.

Pierce had found what he was searching for on the tablet. 'Look.'

Bonner stepped around the graves to join Pierce. He peered at the tablet. On full screen, an old film clip of an early Edwardian city centre was playing. In the busy, packed street people in caps and bowlers and straw hats jostled to and fro, dodging the horse-drawn carts and cabs and omnibuses. In passing, a few of them looked curiously up at whoever was taking the film.

'When I see some interesting looking woman in the crowd, crossing the street or going down some side road, it fascinates me,' said Pierce.

In the film, a woman could be seen moving through the bustling crowd and approaching the camera.

'Like that one. I feel like I want to know her. Want to know where she's going. Want to follow her. Watch her. Find out where she lives. How she lives.'

Bonner stared at Pierce for moment, thinking maybe it was a joke. But Pierce was deadly serious.

'You're just weird,' said Bonner

Pierce ignored the remark. He closed down the tablet. He looked around him at the graveyard, now in semi-darkness. 'So there we are. In a hundred years or so from now it's going to happen. A different kind of interaction, and on a strange scale, but it's going to happen. We've been shown it. You could call it a ticket to time'

'Yeah, well let me tell you something, John.

You've got your maths wrong.'

'Why?'

'Well, if we're assuming the killer is another downtimer...'

'Has to be.'

'Then that makes five of them. But there are only four donors here. Only four people were killed in that crash.'

Pierce thought about this. He then looked once more at the graves.

'Don't worry,' said Bonner. 'Maybe God can tell us what happened.'

Mrs. Pomfret came down the stairs from her flat above the betting shop. She switched on the lights, switched off the security alarm, then unbolted and unlocked the front door for the waiting Bonner and Pierce. She told them of Talbot's visit yesterday, and how the sad pisshead had told her where God lived.

'Somewhere in Princess Mary Road, of all places,' she said. 'I didn't think anyone lived there these days, let alone God.' Having given them all the information she had, she closed the door, re-secured the premises and switched off the lights.

In the darkness of Chain Lane, Bonner took out his mobile. He summoned the team.

20

Shad had packed his few clothes and his belongings, including his Timelight membrane, in a large laundry bag, along with the money and credit cards he had stolen. And now, sitting at Sylvia's dressing table, he was applying some of his healing balm to the wicked looking burn marks that the strands of silk had made on his forearm. He then proceeded to apply more of the shimmering gel to the fine, criss-cross pattern of scar tissue on his chest and upper arms.

The sound of a vehicle outside disturbed him. With the contractors on holiday and the road a virtual dead-end, no-one drove past any more. He pulled on his shirt, switched off the light and hurried out on to the landing and into the darkness of his old bedroom. He moved to the window and peered out and down. He saw a dark coloured hatchback driving slowly past. He assumed that whoever was driving the car had lost their way and reached the dead-end before realising their mistake, and were now driving away. Shifting his angle of view, Shad then saw the car turning and reversing a little further along the road. It then stopped, as if waiting. Its lights were turned off.

Shad moved quickly. He gathered up his healing balm and shoved it in the laundry bag. He then moved down the stairs and into the unlit dining room to peer from the window once more.

Bonner and Pierce watched from inside the parked car. They had driven the length of the road and found that Raymond and Sylvia's house was the only one that looked reasonably clean and had curtains in the windows. And they had seen a crack of light shining from the edge of one set of drawn curtains.

Pierce pulled on protective gloves as he saw the lights of their unmarked police van arriving. It was followed by Allie's SUV. Four fully armed security officers climbed from the van, while Allie and two of her colleagues emerged from the SUV.

Inside the house, Shad had seen the lights of the other vehicles. Still carrying his bag of belongings, he grabbed his coat, making sure the silks were safely in the pocket, then ran out into the back yard.

Bonner knocked loudly on the front door of the B&B. At the same time, Pierce and two of the officers located the rear alleyway to the premises. They entered the yard and saw the open back door of the B&B. Moving carefully inside they then found the bodies of Raymond and Sylvia.

By the time Mrs. O'Day arrived in Princess Mary Road, the house had been searched and yet another call had been put out to the local police, telling them that the missing suspect was still at large and still a danger, and should therefore not be approached by members of the public. A vague description of the man, taken from the evidence given by the landlord and landlady of the Cat in the Cradle pub, was now available and was circulated. Bonner had also asked for the whole of the surrounding area to be cordoned off and searched. 'Could be anywhere in this wilderness,' he had told a grim faced Mrs. O'Day as he showed her around the house.

On seeing the grotesquely arranged bodies of Sylvia and Raymond, Mrs. O'Day, even with all of her experience, was sickened.

'Poor bastards,' she said.

'So what are you going to tell your bosses?' asked Bonner. 'Surely they'll want to know.'

Mrs. O'Day said nothing. They climbed the

stairs to the rooms above and watched Allie and her team at work. Bonner wanted to ask more about Mrs. O'Day's decision, but he decided against it for now. Instead he asked another question, the one that he felt was just as important.

'In the interview room you told the lady that you'd do a deal for the child.'

'No,' said Mrs. O'Day. 'I didn't promise anything. I said, maybe.'

Fran had dropped Jace off at the end of Ferry Lane. As she made her way home she used her mobile to check her landline messages. There was nothing from Bonner. Although she was disappointed by this, she was cheered by the fact that she and Fran had made some good money from the punter. He was a good-looking man in late middle age, and he was considerate and funny, but he just couldn't get it on anymore. So he was happy to have two good looking girls spending time with him, and doing the very best they could for him.

Shad was not hiding out in the wilderness after all. For someone who was adept at moving swiftly, he had made his way through the darkness towards his old haunt, Chain Lane, in the hope of finding somewhere safe to hide. As he walked along Ferry

Lane, with the cloth bag slung over his shoulder, like a sailor from the past, he saw a figure approaching at a distance on the opposite pavement. Wary of being seen, he stopped and hid in the shadows of an archway.

Moving in and out of the light from the streetlamps, the figure approached the barrier that cordoned off part of the demolition site of what was once Dunstall & Sons. As the figure became clearer, Shad was pleased to see that it was a young woman or girl. She clicked along prettily in high heels, and she was wearing a pale blue, shiny plastic coat.

It was almost midnight as Mrs. O'Day and Pierce returned to Charnham Cross. Mrs. O'Day had put herself on standby to wait for news of the downtimer suspect. And right now she had more work to do and further decisions to make. Pierce, who wasn't a great one for sleep, put himself on standby with her. At the same time he was anxious to revisit the Gate Town local history sites on the internet in order to find out even more about the tragedy of nineteen-sixteen-one.

Bonner, on the other hand, was making his weary way home. He had wanted to call on Jace and apologise for not making it today, as planned.

He would have loved to have stayed the night with her so they could put things right. But he still had a wife to go home to. A sexless, marmalade-happy, little old lady of a wife who was only forty-two but crept around in slippers and went to bed in good time, whatever that was.

As he approached his house, which looked unwelcoming with the only sign of life coming from the solitary porch light, he made up his mind to call on Jace first thing in the morning. While turning the key in the lock he reminded himself that Christmas was, thankfully, over and done with. Never mind the twelve sodding days. To his mind, Christmas was now washed up, shafted, finished, kaput, for another twelve months, give or take a mince pie or two.

And thank fuck for that, he thought as he closed the front door.

Jace had been caught by surprise when the multicoloured, luminous silks came spinning towards her from out of the darkness. For just the briefest of moments she had been captivated by their suddenness and by their beauty. And then they had reached her and it was too late.

On the following morning the weather had changed

for the better. It was still cold at half past eight, but the sky was clear and the sun was shining as Bonner stopped at a nearby Co-op and bought a bottle of champagne and a box of fresh cream cakes as a treat. Driving along Ferry Lane he noticed that some of the contractor's vehicles and equipment had returned and a handful of workers were moving parts of the safety barrier that surrounded the demolition site.

Bonner parked near Jace's flat and used the spare keys she had given him to open the street door. He then climbed on up the stairs. Even though Jace had always refused to have overnight punters, he still unlocked and opened the door to the flat quietly just in case. As he did so he experienced a pang of displeasure. He felt, quite wrongly, that this was how a pimp would behave, and the thought made him feel uncomfortable. He liked to think he wasn't the jealous type. After all, this was Jace's work. Well, that was his excuse. Yet in his heart he was relieved that she was planning to give it up.

He set down the champagne and cakes in the small hallway. He then peered through the open door of the living room to find that the curtains were drawn back and the Christmas tree with its fine glass candles was unlit. The flat also felt cold.

And he couldn't imagine Jace entertaining a client in a cold flat.

Thinking maybe she was in the adjoining kitchen, he called out, 'Jace?'

There was no answer. He moved to her bedroom door and eased it open. Once more the curtains were drawn back. And the bed was made. The same applied to the smaller bedroom. A quick glance through the partly opened door of the bathroom revealed that there was no sign of her.

Bonner's guess was that she had probably gone to the shops. So, in order to make their much needed get-together comfy and cosy, he turned up the heating thermostat then gathered up the champagne and cakes and carried them into the living room. He smiled as he saw the two wrapped presents still waiting under the tree. Even though he himself was finished with Christmas, he switched the tree lights on just for this moment of time with Jace, and the grandiose array of glass candles instantly illuminated the room.

From outside, the sound of a pneumatic drill began to fill the air once more. But they didn't bother Bonner. He had grown used to them. He whistled happily to himself as he entered the kitchen. He put the champagne and the cakes in the fridge and opened a cupboard to find glasses and plates. He then stopped as he noticed a fairly bulky laundry bag in the corner of the room. It surprised him. He reckoned a poncy looking laundry bag was definitely not something Jace would bother with. Out of curiosity, he undid the drawstrings of the bag. Inside he could see items of male clothing. Realising that Jace could be with a punter after all, he closed the bag and was all set to make his way quietly out of the kitchen. He then stopped once more, in thought. If she had a punter where was he? And where was she? Then another thought occurred. One that hurt. Has she found someone else? Another lover? If not, why would a punter bring his fucking washing here? He then saw something else that worried him. On a work surface by the sink was Jace's opened purse, loose change, some contact details and house keys. He couldn't believe she would have forgotten her keys. Not Jace.

Erstwhile journeyman Shad *had* found somewhere to hide. It was behind the partly open door of Jace's bathroom. He had waited as Bonner moved around inside the flat. He now reached into his pocket and caressed the silks as he edged his way quietly out from the bathroom and into the hallway.

Still concerned, Bonner walked back into the

living room and looked out of the window, hoping to see Jace returning along Ferry Lane. As he turned from the window the glittering silks came twisting their way through the air towards him. On instinct he ducked and the silks swished past his head and wrapped themselves around the window curtains, slashing them in the process. At the same time Shad entered the room and came rushing at Bonner. Although no mug when it came to defending himself, Bonner was caught completely off guard. He was punched hard in the face, kneed in the groin, then flung across the room with force. He collided with the table, knocking it over with a clatter and a crash of broken ornaments. Half stunned, he managed to regain his balance, but Shad attacked him once more. Again Bonner was hit hard and this time knocked into the tree, where he fell to the floor. Meanwhile Shad had summoned the silks to return to him and with even more speed they were now winging their way towards Bonner. Yet again, Bonner's instinct and training saved him. Although badly hurt, at the last moment he reached up and managed to use the partly fallen tree as a shield. The silks slammed into the brightly lit tree creating mini-explosions of broken glass and blown fuses. This seemed to disorientate the silks, causing them to slash at the tree with what seemed like blind fury before they wrenched themselves free. Then, as if in revenge, they whirled their way back to Shad, ripping at his clothes and tearing open all those old, sad, patched-up wounds of his, making him cry out long and loud with pain. The silks then wrapped themselves around his neck, and, as he sank to his knees, slowly but surely strangled the life out of him.

21

Having blacked out after his injuries, Bonner had missed the sound of the pneumatic drill switching off in Ferry Lane. He had also missed the sounds of emergency vehicles arriving in the lane. When he eventually came to in the hushed comfort of Jace's bedroom he found that he was being patched up by the M.O. from Charnham Cross. Pierce was watching the proceedings. At the same time Allie and her team were in the living room, dealing with the evidence and with the body of Shad.

In his dazed state, Bonner asked anxiously if Jace was home yet. He was relieved to be told by Pierce that she wasn't, because to Bonner this meant she could have been staying out overnight with Fran or another colleague, unaware that a maniac had gained entry to her flat.

When the M.O. had finished, Pierce asked

Bonner if he was fit enough to take a walk with him. Puzzled by this and by Pierce's solemn demeanour, Bonner got up from the bed. Although he had taken a battering, no bones were broken, so he was able to follow Pierce down the stairs and out of the building.

It was then that Bonner saw the emergency vehicles and police officers positioned on and around the demolition site. Pierce stopped and pointed in the direction of the dusty, rubble strewn site.

Bonner began to realise that the worst had happened as he walked to the site and picked his way through what was left of Dunstall & Sons' yard, where the motor coaches had once waited on an August day long ago. And Bonner remembered that he was last here just before Christmas, when he had set out to rescue Jace from the unsafe building but had to be rescued by her instead. He recalled seeing her in the pale blue PVC coat high up at the top of the structure in the winter sunshine.

And now, as he ducked under the police marker tapes in today's cold sunlight he saw the blue coat again. This time it was lying, with other items of clothing, some distance from a covered body. He reached the body, pulled back the covering, not fearing, but knowing full well what he would find, and looked down at the young girl-like body of Jace. He knelt down in the dust and debris and gently touched the terrible wounds on her throat. He then eased his arms under her, held her body close to him and kissed her dead face.

As he eventually got to his feet he found that Mrs. O'Day was standing beside him.

'Sorry about your friend. Really sorry.'

She saw tears in Bonner's eyes. She then surprised him by reaching forward, grabbing him and hugging him in what could best be described as a man-to-man bear hug. There was nothing ladylike about that hug.

'I'm on your side, Sol,' she said. 'Always have been. Always will be.' She rocked him to and fro for a moment or two before releasing him. 'Now go home, get yourself cleaned up. Then rest. Take some time off.'

Right now, Bonner was having trouble trying to get his thoughts together, yet he was conscious of a change in Mrs. O'Day's demeanour. There was a calmness about her. And a sense of purpose. But inside him there was still anger. And sorrow.

'Things aren't finished,' he managed to mutter.

'Of course they're finished,' she replied. 'You finished it. You helped to kill the bastard.' She turned and saw Pierce waiting at a distance. 'By the way, John found the fifth grave at the Connaught. It's not that far away from the other graves. It's just that the date was different. That confused him.'

'What do you mean, the date was different? What date?'

'He didn't die in the crash. He died because of it.'

Gate Town Gazette – Friday September 8, 1961 – Obituaries
Michael Oliver Dunstall
Exactly one month from the day of the fatal company coach crash, Michael Dunstall, youngest of the Dunstall brothers and co-director of the well established local company Dunstall & Sons, sadly took his own life…

Even though friends and relatives had tried their best to persuade him otherwise, Mr. Michael, who was in charge of the second coach, had blamed himself for the crash and had never mentally recovered from the events of that terrible day.

It was to be the last of the renowned Dunstall & Sons outings. But then, the days of the company itself were already numbered. In a few years technological advances by rival firms would put paid to Dunstall's overstaffed and old fashioned business methods. Then for many years the building was used as temporary workshops and storage facilities for a number of back street outfits before being partly wrecked by squatters and set fire to by deadbeats until its eventual demise.

Lesley was pottering around in the kitchen as Bonner arrived home. Still behaving like someone's dippy grandmother, she gave his bruised and battered face just the briefest of glances.

'Oh, you've hurt yourself. I'll make you a cup of tea.'

'No, thanks,' he replied.

He retired to the living room, poured himself a scotch and downed it in one. He looked around him at the room with its tidy fussiness and its abundance of bits and bobs and tasteless knick-knacks. It had been Lesley's choice in everything from the outset. He had never had a say in how their home should look because he had never really been bothered. He had left it all to her. But now he found himself thinking about the crazy beauty of Jace's little flat and how he would miss her and everything about her.

'Jace!' he cried in a loud, hurt voice, not caring whether or not Lesley heard him. Because it didn't matter. Not now. He leant back in his chair and poured another scotch. He then closed his eyes and fell asleep before he could drink it.

Bonner awoke in his armchair just after six-thirty p.m. He had experienced a jumble of uneasy dreams about gravestones and whirling silks, interspersed with half-awake memories of Jace. And, despite Mrs. O'Day's reassurances, things were not finished as far as he was concerned. He'd lost the person he'd loved. And there were still downtimers here, albeit under lock and key. So there were still questions to be answered.

He eased his aching body out of the chair and went to the bathroom to douse his face with cold water. He could hear Lesley happily busying herself in the kitchen. But he couldn't cope with talking to her. Not right now. Pulling on his coat, he left the house and into the cold night air. He started his car and headed out of Gate Town.

Thin clouds interspersed with moonlight shifted across the sky as Bonner arrived at Charnham Cross. Although lights were on in the camp and a couple of vehicles were parked in the courtyard, the gates were closed but not manned. So Bonner parked his car on the grass verge before swiping in his security ID card to gain access. As the gates automatically closed shut after him, he walked across the courtyard and entered the building. The place was empty. He called out, but there was no reply. He walked behind the reception desk and tapped in Mrs. O'Day's number. The line was dead.

None of it made sense to Bonner as he walked along empty corridors. He called out once more. But there was still no reply. He climbed stairs to Mrs. O'Day's dark office. He switched on the light. The desk held its usual array of paperwork but there was no sign of his boss.

Worried now, Bonner walked quickly through the building to the old hospital wing. The door to the side ward was open. Bonner peered in. Eve and her daughter were no longer there.

Bonner hurried back from the hospital wing and climbed the iron stairs to the cell block. Once more he called out, his voice echoing along the gantries. Still no reply. He moved to the door of David Doughty's cell. That, too, was open. And Doughty had gone. Hearing footsteps approaching along the gantry, Bonner turned to look. It was Allie.

'Allie, what the hell's going on? Where is everyone?'

'Most of them have left, Sir. There's a couple of guards still patrolling. That's all.'

'What d'you mean, they've left?'

'Sent home.'

'So where are the downtimers?'

'Mrs. O'Day and Inspector Pierce, they've taken them.'

'Taken them where?'

'To the Connaught cemetery.'

Bonner couldn't believe what he'd heard. 'Jesus Christ!' he said. 'Why there of all places?'

Allie noticed his injured face. 'She said it was to do with the graves.'

'Those fucking graves again? Why?'

'I've no idea. She wouldn't tell me. All I could make out was that they're in danger.'

'Who's in danger?'

'The downtimers.'

Bonner thought about this. He remembered the conversation in the Walholme hotel and Mrs. O'Day's palpable concern about possible plans being made by her bosses. He took out his mobile.

'It's no good ringing her,' said Allie. 'Her phone's off.'

Bonner put his mobile back in his pocket. 'When did she leave?'

'Not long ago. You must have just missed them.' She stared at his injuries once more. 'Look at you. Look at your poor face.' She wanted to reach out and touch his face, but thought better of it. 'The last victim, Sir. I hear you were close to her.'

'Yes,' said Bonner. 'I was.'

He turned and moved quickly back along the gantry. Allie hurried after him.

'Where are you going?'

'Where d'you think?'

Bonner and Allie descended the stairs of the cellblock. Bonner then stopped on the landing as the walls of the stairwell were suddenly illuminated by the reflected lights of approaching vehicles. He moved to the window and looked out.

'Mrs. O'Day was right,' he said. 'They are in danger.'

Allie joined him at the window. She, too, looked out and saw a convoy of vehicles moving at speed towards them along the track road.

Bonner and Allie stepped out from the administration building. Bonner then drew back as he saw the vehicles coming to a halt outside the gates. The limousine of Mrs. O'Day's nameless visitor was there once more, followed by the black Range Rover. But on this occasion there was a third vehicle making up the convoy. It was a prisoner transport van.

Bonner took Allie's arm as they kept in the shadow of the building and proceeded to ease their way along the outside wall away from the entrance.

As the limo driver sounded his horn, security men in their smart black suits climbed from the Range Rover and tried to open the locked gates. Having no success, one of them waved to the driver of the Range Rover. The men then moved clear of the gates as the Range Rover swung out from behind the limo and drove its heavy bull bars hard into the gates, bursting them open. Men and vehicles then proceeded to move through the gates.

As Bonner and Allie hid and watched, the visitor climbed from the limousine.

'Mister smarm and charm,' said Bonner quietly.

Allie was puzzled. 'Who?'

'It doesn't matter.'

They continued to watch as the visitor and most of his men hurried inside the building, leaving two of the security team to keep watch. At that moment the two Charnham Cross guards appeared on the far side of the courtyard. One of the security men took an automatic pistol from a holster hidden inside his black jacket. He aimed the gun at the two guards.

'You stay put!' the security man called to them. 'Move and you're dead!'

The two guards stayed put.

'We have to get out of here somehow,' Bonner whispered.

'We can't.' Allie pointed across the courtyard. 'My car's over there. But we'll never get past them.'

'Mine's parked outside the gates. We'll have to go the long way round.'

'What about the fences?' said Allie.

'Do you have keys?'

Allie tapped her pocket. 'Yes.'

'Good. Come on!'

Keeping in the shadows, he took her arm once more and edged along the shadowed wall. They eventually reached the end of the building and were out of the shadows. And now the second security man had seen them.

'You there!' the man shouted. 'Stay where you are!'

But Bonner and Allie ignored the command as they ran in the direction of the old parade ground. Fine big Allie, built like an Olympian, easily outpaced Bonner.

'Where are we heading?' she called as they ran.

'The compounds,' said Bonner.

Other security men had emerged from the administration building and were giving chase. But they were some way behind. As Bonner and Allie reached the smaller compound, Bonner, a little out of breath, pointed at the gate. Allie took a set of keys from her pocket, juggled with them in the darkness, then accidentally dropped them.

'For fuck's sake!' said Bonner, puffing and glancing round at the pursuing figures.

Allie managed to find the keys. She unlocked the gate and she and Bonner entered quickly, locking the gate to after them.

'Far side,' said Bonner.

As they ran through the assorted shapes and colours of the activity centre Bonner grabbed the ladder-like climbing frame and wrenched it from the wooden tower. They then continued to the far side of the compound where Bonner shoved the climbing frame against the fence. Behind them, the security men had reached the locked gate and were kicking at it.

Allie was no helpless female. She climbed the frame like an athlete and Bonner had a momentary glimpse of those wonderful legs as she swung them over the fence before lowering herself to the ground. His scaling of the fence was more scrambled and less elegant, but he made it. The two of them then ran on, under the overhanging branches of trees, as the security men finished breaking down the compound gate.

Bonner and Allie continued running along the edge of the complex until they reached the main gates. On hearing a babble of voices from outside the admin building, they crouched low as they manoeuvred their way to Bonner's car.

Still in a crouched position, Bonner eased open the driver's door. Allie did likewise at the front passenger side. Not having locked the vehicle, there was no flash from the hazard warning lights to give them away. Once inside the car they peered out to see dark suited figures illuminated by the courtyard lights.

'This is no speed machine,' said Bonner as he inserted the key into the ignition. 'But we'll try to get as far ahead of the buggers as we can.'

He left the lights off as he started the ignition. He then swung the car quickly in reverse.

'They've seen us,' said Allie as she watched the figures in the courtyard.

'OK. Hold tight.'

Bonner turned the wheel, revved up and drove off fast into the darkness of the track road before switching on his lights.

At the same time the limousine and the Range Rover drivers started their engines. In a hurry, they turned their vehicles in the courtyard but had to wait as the prisoner transport van that blocked the entrance was driven to one side. Leaving the van behind, the Range Rover, followed by the limo, sped off in pursuit of Bonner's car.

PJ Hammond

Bonner was right. There had been a change in Mrs. O'Day's demeanour. Early in the afternoon she had received an email that said, 'Situation reviewed. Changes imminent. Acknowledge receipt of this message immediately.'

Mrs. O'Day had given no such acknow-ledgement. After deleting the message and closing down her computer, she had blocked all incoming landline and mobile calls to Charnham Cross before sending home almost all of the staff that had been recalled on Boxing Day, including nurse Claire.

Pierce had brought all of Shad's belongings to Mrs. O'Day's office. She then explained the plans she had made as she and Pierce locked the silks, the membrane and the gel sachets inside a small metal case.

David Doughty had been relieved of his gardening duties and returned to his quarters. Then, as the late afternoon sky began to darken, Mrs. O'Day made her way along now deserted corridors to the side ward to ask Eve further questions about the Timelight procedure.

Troubled by the urgency in Mrs. O'Day's voice, Eve had answered what questions she could, but explained that the basic system was of no use to scientists of the present day should they wish to capture donors from their own past, because the technology lay in the future. Mrs. O'Day told her that that particular aspect of the system was of no interest to her.

'What is wrong?' Eve had asked, nervously, holding Cara close to her. 'What is happening?'

'You'll know soon enough,' was all Mrs. O'Day would say.

And now, as Bonner pushed his poor hatchback to its limits along the dual carriageway and into the lights of Gate Town, Eve found herself being led from the Charnham Cross staff car to the open gates of the Connaught cemetery. Patchy moonlight and the gleam from a solitary torch revealed that Mrs. O'Day was leading the way. Eve followed her, clutching the hand of Cara who was wrapped in a warm coat. Next was David Doughty. Last in line was Pierce. He carried the metal case and a slim document bag.

Bonner had planned to lead the pursuers a merry dance around the back streets of Gate Town in an attempt to lose them. But he reckoned if they were to warn Mrs. O'Day, they would have lost time. And at least his madcap drive had gained some advantage. Although not enough.

As they drove through the lane where the schoolgirl had died they saw the staff car parked up ahead of them. On reaching the cemetery they climbed from the car. Allie pointed towards the main pathway.

'There.'

Bonner looked. In the semi-darkness the small procession could be seen making its way along the pathway.

'What the fuck is she up to?' said Bonner as he and Allie ran through the open gate and along the pathway.

Up ahead the group had reached the narrow grass path that led to the graves of the coach crash victims. As Bonner and Allie reached them Mrs. O'Day, the torch carrier, stopped and turned.

'I told you to go home and rest,' she said.

'Rest?' said Bonner angrily. 'What is all this? What's going on? And why wasn't I told?'

'You wouldn't have understood…'

'You bet your fucking life I wouldn't have understood…'

'Therefore you would have got in the way.'

'Well, don't worry. There'll be a few more people getting in the way quite soon.' He indicated the road. 'Your boss has arrived. Team handed.'

'Sorry, Ma'am,' said Allie. 'We had to come. Had to tell you.'

Mrs. O'Day glanced towards the road, then

back. 'Then we'd better get a move on.'

She directed the torch beam as she shepherded the three downtimers along the grass path.

'Hey, hold on,' said Bonner as he followed them. 'At least tell us what you're doing, for Christ's sake.'

'I'm going to try to send them back.'

'What?' Bonner was mystified, and still angry. 'This is fucking crazy!'

Mrs. O'Day ignored him as she led the group on along the path.

'And what about the stuff that murdering bastard brought with him?' Bonner shouted.

'It's going back with them,' said Pierce as he eased his way past Bonner. 'It doesn't belong here. Not in our time.'

Further along the grass path, Mrs. O'Day had stopped. She began to arrange Eve, Cara and Doughty in a line beside the graves. Pierce handed Doughty the metal case. Pierce then unzipped the document bag, and, with great care, removed the membrane that was once hidden in Cara's pencil box. As the colours and shapes began to emerge, he handed the membrane to Eve before he and Mrs. O'Day stepped quickly back along the path and out of range.

Bonner looked towards the road. He then

turned to Allie with a look of exasperation. She gave a shrug.

Eve held the membrane tilted slightly and at chest height as the colours and figures and vehicles in the Ferry Lane yard of 1961 now danced and weaved and floated their way around the cemetery. Mrs. O'Day and Pierce watched and waited as the moving shapes highlighted headstones, columns, urns, decorative angels, real flowers, plastic flowers and name after name after name of the dead.

But nothing happened…

Bonner was even more exasperated. He moved along the path to join Mrs. O'Day.

'There isn't time for this,' he said. 'All this lost souls crap. How do you expect it to work?'

Mrs. O'Day indicated the glary old Kodak camera pictures that continued to circle around them. 'We're seeing some of it.'

'No,' said Bonner. 'We're seeing a projected image. One that's way past our understanding…'

'Listen to me, Sol…'

'But still an image. Nothing more…'

'Just fucking listen. Because I'm just as sceptical as you are about all this…'

'Then call it off…'

'A small ghost.'

'What?'

'She told us, remember? That's why the child travelled back with her. She had to bring her. The donors have to more or less match.'

'Oh, for Christ's sake!'

Mrs. O'Day raised her voice, angry with him. 'I said, fucking listen to me.'

Bonner shut up as Mrs. O'Day continued. 'Some poxy beam of light from some poxy fucking future, that's suppose to come here and carry people away, of course I'm fucking sceptical. But I have to try it. I have to see if it does bloody work.' She looked at the three forlorn figures that still waited by the graves. 'Because, after five killings by some psychopath from another time, they stand no chance. My bosses will get all the information they need from them, by fair means or foul, and then dispose of them. That's why this has to work. For their sakes.'

And still nothing happened…

Bonner pointed towards Eve. 'But even she said this system of theirs was hit and miss.'

'Yet she arrived. She and her child and the others arrived.'

'And isn't it supposed to be an event that brings them back?' Bonner argued. 'She told us that. Nothing grand. Nothing big. Just an event. All right, so it's sad what happened all those years ago. But people die in crashes every fucking day. Why should their deaths be any different?'

'Sir?' called Allie, as she pointed towards the road.

Bonner turned and saw the headlights of approaching vehicles.

'Too late,' he said to Mrs. O'Day. But as he spoke to her he thought he saw three faint shapes, illuminated by the shifting images, yet not a part of them. These shapes were motionless and they seemed to be standing alongside Eve, Cara and Doughty.

Car doors slammed from outside the gates as the security personnel emerged from their vehicles. Surprised momentarily by the dancing images, they then switched on torches and entered the cemetery.

'Mrs. O'Day!' the visitor's voice called out. 'Stop whatever you're doing! Return those people!'

He and his men began to move quickly along the main pathway and grass verges, their figures mingling with the shifting, dancing Kodak images of long ago.

Yet again, nothing happened...

'So what *exactly* do they want?' asked Bonner. 'What is the danger?'

'I've already told you,' said Mrs. O'Day. She

gazed up at the night sky as the paint-box images flickered across her face. 'They get what they want by whatever means. And they want our downtimers. Especially the child. They want her eyes.'

'What?' Bonner was horrified. He looked towards the small lost figure of Cara and her frightened mother.

'Well the bastards have won,' he said as the pursuers reached the grass pathway and closed in on them. 'They've fucking won.'

And then it came…

It was not a single shaft of light but three vividly blue narrow beams. And they came not from high above, but as if from some point just above the horizon.

The visitor and his men were stopped in their tracks as it swept above them. Fearing some sort of attack, they instinctively took cover behind headstones as the beams dipped and flew low over the cemetery, while Pierce and Allie threw themselves to the ground.

But Bonner and Mrs. O'Day, shocked and alarmed, stayed watching. They saw the beams hit the small group waiting by the graves. Then the membrane images were extinguished as the beams of light suddenly withdrew at enormous speed to that strange horizon, before instantly disappearing.

Bonner and Mrs. O'Day moved towards the graves then stopped abruptly and stared in amazement.

Eve, Cara and Doughty were no longer there. In their place remained the faint shapes of the three matching donors, Dunstall & Sons' day trippers, Karen, her son Noel and Mr. Michael, still in 1961, yet somehow together, and for all time. They could be seen for a moment or two more before fading from sight.

The End

Printed in Great
Britain
by Amazon